THE LYNCH PARTY

Pete Hadfield had been ordered by his father to bring in his half-brother, Harry, who stood accused of murder. However, Harry had always denied his guilt and it was up to Pete to prove his brother's innocence even though he thought the case against him was too strong. Pete had to take drastic action and before long he was heading for a lynch party. Only his determination could save Harry . . .

F
LP RA   THE
LYNCH PARTY   GULLIVER

100%
recycled paper

MARTIN GULLIVER

◆

THE LYNCH PARTY

Complete and Unabridged

LINFORD
Leicester

First hardcover edition published in
Great Britain in 2002
Originally published in paperback as
'Shadow of a Noose' by Wes Yancey

First Linford Edition
published 2003
by arrangement with
Robert Hale Limited, London

British Library CIP Data

Gulliver, Martin
    The lynch party.—Large print ed.—
Linford western library
1. Western stories
2. Large type books
I. Title II. Yancey, Wes. Shadow of a noose
813.5′4 [F]

ISBN 1–8439–5080–4

Published by
F. A. Thorpe (Publishing)
Anstey, Leicestershire

Set by Words & Graphics Ltd.
Anstey, Leicestershire
Printed and bound in Great Britain by
T. J. International Ltd., Padstow, Cornwall

This book is printed on acid-free paper

1

The Reckless One

They had been riding all day across the vast, silent country, seeing no other living soul. There were only sidewinders that moved warily in rocky clefts at the approach of the two horses, and, in the distance, gliding buzzards. The two men had covered twenty miles since dawn. For one of them it had been an ordeal. His wrists were tied firmly with cord and he was able to grasp the reins only with his fingers.

Sweat and dust emphasised the grim lines of his face. He had tried to escape twice, knowing from the start of each attempt that it was futile with this quiet, determined man behind him. Now he was tired and wanted to conserve his strength. Anyway, before the sun went down behind the

Sacramento Mountains, in this western area of Texas, they would reach their destination. And then there'd be hell to pay!

Now he was thirsty.

'How about some water, brother mine?' The man with the tied hands jerked his animal to a halt and stared mockingly at his captor.

Pete Hadfield halted his gelding and gave Harry a long, patient look. The roughly defined trail through the shallow canyon had first been used by bands of passing Comanche and then by wandering riders. There was evidence that a wheeled wagon had passed through a long time back. The hills were of redstone, bare at the peaks, with soil thick enough on the lower slopes to maintain clumps of browned grama grass and cholla cactus and an occasional Joshua tree. Sheep had been through the land, herded probably by Mexicans. Now silence lay heavily over the great valleys and hills.

'Are you tryin' to be smart again?'

2

Pete asked. His eyes, shaded by the dusty stetson, were narrowed and wary. His shirt was stained at the front where sweat and dust had mixed. His yellow bandanna looked like a rag. 'You had water only three miles back. Maybe you're figurin' to make a play, Harry, now that we're gettin' to the end of the trail?'

'No play,' Harry said. 'You got all the cards, Pete.' He licked at his dry lips and spat out the gritty mixture. 'You got guns, water, grub — and righteousness. Me, I'm just a no-good skunk. You know it — I know it — and pa knows it best of all. The truth is, I need some water. C'mon, Pete, we're not short . . . '

'All right. I won't deny you water.' Pete Hadfield unstrapped one of the canteens from the cantle. He jigged his horse closer and he held out the uncorked canteen. Harry raised it to his lips and drank deep. Then, his dust mask cracking with his old, reckless smile, he handed back the canteen.

'Here, brother! You have a drink. Go ahead, relax! You know, old sobersides, there ain't many men who would figure us for brothers . . . '

'We're only half-brothers,' said Pete quietly.

'Yeah . . . our old pa took himself two wives in quick succession and sired us just as fast. Then his second wife died and he became a hard old cuss and still is. Say, are you gonna drink or do you figure this ride to be some kind of test? You seem to regard everything like one big duty, brother of mine: Duty to pa, duty to me, duty to the ranch, even to the damned steers in the valleys! Why don't you kick up like me? Get some fun out of life before it's too late, Pete!'

Pete tipped the canteen back for a drink. Momentarily his eyes were off his brother. Harry Hadfield was ready. He kicked his feet free of the stirrups and leaped. His tied hands clawed for Pete's arms and gained a hold. The sudden attack sent the water bottle spinning and knocked Pete Hadfield off balance.

4

Harry fell from his saddle, between the horses, and his weight brought Pete down with him.

As the animals pranced about in sudden fright, the two men wrestled on the warm shale and red soil. Harry's bound hands placed him at a real disadvantage. He knew he had to pull a fast trick if this move was to produce anything but more sweat. He kicked at his half-brother, a high-heeled riding boot that hacked across Pete's shins. Then Harry's bunched hands swung viciously at Pete's face, landing and scraping a bruise down one cheek. Pete Hadfield rolled clear, got to his feet and advanced on Harry. He didn't draw his gun.

As Harry scrambled to his knees, Pete swung a right. His fist connected and Harry fell back, a glazed expression in his dark eyes. Pete Hadfield grabbed him and then shook him hard.

'Look, you crazy cuss! Pa told me to go out and get you — and I've done just that! Don't you try any more fool tricks, Harry! Do you want to provide some fun for a lynch-party or are you gonna come quietly with me to the ranch and then to the jail at Perkinsville? That way you'll get a fair trial. You've got a crazy story and only Judge Harlan can decide what to do with a galoot who killed Polly Bliss.'

Harry Hadfield heard only part of the outburst. His mocking smile was proof of that. His curved lips held the smile as his bound hands groped for a hefty stone. With Pete only lightly holding his shoulders he made another desperate play. His hands jerked up, the stone cupped in them. The hard smooth rock rammed into Pete's chin, a blow that would have shaken a professional fighter. Pete swayed back, his hands losing the faint grip. Blood suddenly appeared on his chin. The bruise from the first blow showed red and angry beside the yellow trail dust on his face. As Pete swayed dazedly, Harry scrambled back and then kicked out at his half-brother, the sole of his boot crashing against his jaw. Pete Hadfield rolled over and lay still.

The oldster with the gun seemed to appear from nowhere. Ten yards away his docile burro stood in a small cavelike recess. The old man held the .45 as if it was a small cannon.

'Hold it, you two! Seen you comin' for miles. Now don't I know you gents from somewheres?'

'I'm Harry Hadfield . . . I'm known in Perkinsville . . . '

'Yep. Seen you in the saloons. Hadfield, huh? That's the name of the owner of the TT outfit . . . '

'My pa,' said Harry quickly. 'Hey, you got a knife? Sure you have! Just cut these damned cords, will you?'

'Not so durned fast, *hombre*!' the old man shrilled. 'Now why were you two fightin'? Who's this other feller? Why are you tied up anyway?'

'He's no pal of mine, old-timer,' said Harry. 'Now if you start cuttin' I'm willin' to pay you plenty.'

The old fellow rubbed his left hand

uncertainly over his whiskery face and looked down at the prone man. 'Say, you really hit him! Now he's stirrin' though. Must be plenty tough after the way you slammed him with that stone! Reminds me of a galoot I knew in Arizona who used to prizefight with stones in his fists . . . '

'C'mon, cut me loose!' Harry urged. His grim face an ugly mask, he stepped towards the old man.

The Colt jerked up and the oldster's eyes gleamed brightly. 'You got some dinero? I'm broke! All I got is food and water, and not much of that either — '

'Sure, I've got money! In my belt! Cut these goddamn cords, old man, before he gets to his feet! Now!'

The old prospector suddenly made up his mind. He stepped close to Harry Hadfield, brought out a Bowie knife and sliced through the wrist bindings. Harry went to the groaning Pete, snicked out the gun from the holster and rammed it into his empty leather. Then he turned to the two horses. The animals had wandered away a few yards and were standing there uncertainly. As Harry rushed to them, one horse shied. But Harry Hadfield was interested in the animal that carried the water canteen and the rifles in the saddle scabbard. He reached the big black gelding, grabbed its leathers and vaulted into the saddle.

The old man blinked angrily. 'Hey, what about my dinero?' The horse's hoofs began to drum. The oldster let out a string of curses and then fired his .45. But Harry Hadfield, with the luck of his kind, was a jerking, receding target. After two shots, the old-timer gave up and threw oaths to the blue skies.

'Guess you've lost out, mister,' muttered a voice, and the old man turned to look at Pete Hadfield who was getting groggily to his feet.

'That pesky devil done tricked me . . . '

'Well, if it's any consolation you're not the first,' said Pete gruffly. 'You should've known better.'

'He promised me money.'

'Harry is good at promises.'

'You tied him up, huh? Why?'

'He's my brother and he's a murderer,' said Pete wearily. 'I had orders to bring him in. Now help me round up the other horse, old man — it's the least you can do!'

'Sure. You goin' to Perkinsville? I'd be mighty glad of company . . . '

'No, I'm heading for the TT spread — my father's outfit.'

'He's your brother, huh? And he's killed some galoot?'

'A woman — a single girl in Perkinsville,' said Pete grimly. 'There are men in town who'd like to string him up without a trial.'

Pete strode off angrily, his gaze fixed on the distant horse. The animal was a brown mare, hardy but not as big-boned as the black gelding. The two horses were from the TT remuda, but the big black had been Pete's favourite mount. And the saddle had been a special job.

The wary brown mare lifted its head as he approached slowly, losing interest in the clump of brownish grass. Pete gathered up the reins and climbed into the saddle. Bitterly he glanced at the empty saddle scabbard. The rig consisted of only a blanket and a lariat. Harry had been in a hurry when he had left the TT two days ago. Maybe he had figured to cross the border at El Paso but he had made the mistake of lingering too long at a hillside spring. Pete had jumped him and then disarmed him. Now there were two rifles in the scabbard on the black. Pete had thrown Harry's sixgun into the brush a long way back.

Pete Hadfield urged the horse forward and went down the slope; heading westward, into the sun. The oldster appeared with his burro. 'Hey, mister, reckon I'll ride along with you!'

Pete smiled faintly. 'You aim to make it a long ride, old man? That critter is the slowest thing I've seen!'

'Well, we'll get there! Now what're

you in such a hurry for? That brother of yours has got clear away — and maybe it's for the better, huh?'

Pete nodded. 'Could be you're right. Pa gave me one helluva chore riding out after my own brother, though it isn't the first time pa and I have had to get him out of trouble. Fool of a cuss! Drinking sprees — gambling — women. He rode with Duke Malden for a spell, then he disappeared from the ranch and Perkinsville for about two months. I figure they held up stages, but I don't know for sure. Duke got killed and Harry came wanderin' back home as if nothin' was wrong. The law never got onto him . . . '

'Knowed a few wild 'uns like that,' said the old-timer. 'Best to let 'em have their heads, like an ornery horse. They either end up dead or they cool off. Say, he told me he was Harry Hadfield! I reckon I seen him in the saloons in Perkinsville.'

'I'm Pete — Hadfield,' said the young man. 'My pa runs the TT outfit ten miles this side of town.'

'I'm Jo-Jo. Name's Joe Johanson, but all the galoots I ever knowed always called me Jo-Jo.'

'You been prospecting?'

'Yep. There's gold somewheres at the tail end of the Sacramento hills, I seen sign and I got me a poke of nuggets out of the stream that runs to the Pecos River, but it ain't all that much . . . '

'Jo-Jo, that damned burro will take all night to get to the ranch,' said Pete in exasperation. 'I've got to leave you. I've got to tell Pa that Harry has taken off, and I need guns . . . '

'To chase your own brother?'

'That's right, old — '

His words were cut off by the faint bark of handgun shots. The shots came from the distance and only the silence of the land allowed them to be heard.

2

'I Didn't Kill the Girl!'

Pete Hadfield kept the brown mare at a full gallop until the animal got wild-eyed and then he slowed down the pace and sent the animal down into a valley of yellowish sand. Pete urged the mare into a scrambling climb up a scrub-filled slope, its haunches working like big springs. At the top of the rim he reined up and stared into the depression below. A mile away redstone buttes rose abruptly from the arid land, but Pete Hadfield had eyes only for the scene below.

Harry had been cornered. But he had been lucky again and was uninjured, although one man of the party was holding a bloodied arm and cursing.

Pete recognized the four men immediately: Big Ben Link, the blacksmith

14

from Perkinsville; Josh Hardy, head freight driver with Purdy Lines; Mick Laverty, an ex-deputy who had broken a few laws himself; and young Wally Bliss, brother of the girl who'd been found dead.

The man with the wounded arm was Josh Hardy and he looked up as Pete rode towards them. 'Hey, here's the other one! Two Hadfields, by hell!'

'Steady!' warned Big Ben Link. 'We've got no argument with Pete Hadfield, just with this damned brother of his! And we've found him, by thunder!'

'I knew he'd head for these waste-lands,' said Wally Bliss.

'You knew?' sneered Mick Laverty, his sallow face betraying some Mexican ancestry. 'He's had enough time to be past El Paso, but that don't matter a hoot right now. We've got the lousy killer, so let's find a tree and string him up. There ain't no need to be bothered with Sheriff Sharkey, or Judge Harlan!'

The four men were edgy as a result of

two days of hard riding and only Ben Link was a steadying influence. He was built like a railroad navvy and was as bald as an egg under his battered hat. His thick thighs filled his brown cord pants and he wore a Colt; it was unusual to see Ben Link with a gun. He was a married man, with a daughter who had been friendly with Polly Bliss, and that was one reason why he was riding with these vengeful men. Mick Laverty, Pete knew, had had visions of leading Polly to the altar, even though he hadn't received the slightest encouragement, not even a dance with the girl at the church hall. He had just hung around, pestering Polly if the truth be known. He had hated Harry Hadfield when he saw Polly dance with Harry all night before going riding with him the next day.

Josh Hardy had gone along with Big Ben Link, full of indignation over the rumour that Harry Hadfield had killed Polly Bliss. Josh, with iron-grey hair and a weathered face, was now regretting joining this manhunt. A wounded arm meant time off from work and he couldn't afford it.

Wally Bliss, like Mick Laverty, was thirsting for revenge, and every indication of an ugly character was revealed in his face. It was strange that Polly had been as pretty as a picture while Wally Bliss owned a surly mouth, a bent nose and mean little eyes. He was a small man of about twenty-five, clad in a dirty shirt and a black leather vest. He waved his gun about as if ready to wipe out a pack of marauding Comanches.

'How about it? Are we lynching the rat?' said Mick Laverty.

'You ought to know better than that,' Ben Link rasped. 'You worked with the sheriff.'

'I say string him up!' shrilled Wally Bliss. 'I go along with Mick! Ain't that why we rode along these stinkin' hot canyons? We figured to hang him right from the jump!'

'I never said that!' Ben Link turned his horse to the young man. 'And put that hogleg away, Wally! You could drill one of us the way you hold that iron.'

'He killed my sister! The dirty coyote. I've a mind to plug him right now!' The gun shook as rage possessed him.

Pete Hadfield rode the mare into the group. Coming level with Wally Bliss, he whipped a hand out and grabbed the man's gun wrist and twisted. Wally yelped in pain and the gun fell. Pete thrust the arm away and rowelled his mare back to stare grimly at the other men.

'There'll be no neck-tie party!'

'That skunk killed little Polly!' Mick Laverty shouted. 'He was never good enough for her, the skunk! Sure, he had money — stolen money, I'd guess. And he was full of smart talk! Tryin' to impress her, show her how big he was! I know him! He picked up a lot of gun tricks with Duke Malden and I reckon he should be just as dead as that rotten outlaw!'

'Give me a gun,' said Harry Hadfield coolly, 'and you can say all that again at a distance of twenty yards, face to face.'

'You'll hang!' said the other vehemently. 'Here or in town!'

Harry Hadfield sat on the black calmly, his brain racing over the possibilities available to him. Big Ben Link had disarmed him, had taken the handgun and the two rifles after Josh Hardy had been nicked. It had been bad luck running into these Perkinsville men and would not have happened if Pete had not brought him back over the trail. And what now? Once again a break for freedom had run into a dead-end.

'Too much durned yap,' grunted Big Ben Link. 'We're headin' back. There'll be no shootin' and no doggone hangin'. You'll see a judge and a jury in town, Harry Hadfield, and may God help you!'

'That's all we want,' said Pete.

'I take it you've been after this brother of yours?'

'I found him up near the old Comanche trail. I was bringin' him back but he escaped.'

Wally Bliss nudged his horse around. His lopsided face was full of hate. 'That's a pack of lies. I figure you was tryin' to help him get away.'

'You can say what the hell you like,' said Pete grimly. 'You're full of hate. Look, Ben Link, I'm ridin' with you to make sure Harry reaches town alive. That's all I ask.'

'Oh, boy, brother mine!' mocked Harry. 'I wish I had your high moral values. There's only one thing wrong . . . '

'And what the heck is that?'

'No one wants to believe me when I say I didn't kill the girl!' Harry took up the reins and turned on his reckless, mirthless grin. 'Not even you, Pete, or pa! It's mighty strange, even to a crazy galoot like me, when no one accepts my word — so I'll say it again, loud and clear, just for the hell of it. I didn't kill Polly Bliss!'

'You lyin' skunk!' yelled Wally, and he rowelled his horse straight at the black.

For some moments there was confusion as frightened horses bumped each other and, neighing shrilly, heads high, twisted around. But Pete rode on one side of Harry and Ben Link nudged his mount along the other side. The two angry men had to be content to make a lot of verbal noise and eventually they simmered down. Then Ben Link shouted orders angrily. Josh Hardy, holding his arm, glowered from his saddle, as Pete Hadfield fixed grim eyes on his half-brother. Harry, maintaining his mocking smile, waited.

'Let's ride back to town!' shouted Ben Link.

Horses were pointed west and urged into a canter. As the party went past the redstone buttes, old Joe Johanson rode his burro into the valley and glared at the departing riders.

'Now this sure beats all! It's gettin' kind of crowded out here. Seems them Hadfields have sure met up with plenty of company. Don't look like they figger I count at all, but all the same I aim to head in that direction.'

But Joe Johanson didn't make it to Perkinsville that night. The burro was slow and old and twice it decided to halt and hang its head, refusing to budge. The party of riders trotted weary horses into town just as the oil lamps were lit at the street corners and the saloons got the first evening customers. Harry Hadfield was shoved into the jail by Mick Laverty, who acted as though he still wore a badge. Sheriff Tom Sharkey was away, in the boomtown of Alpine, identifying two wanted men, and that had been why the unofficial posse had gone off in search of Harry Hadfield. A wire had been sent to the hotel at Alpine, informing the sheriff of the murder, but there was no one to represent the law in town. Judge Harlan was off on his circuit. No doubt he'd hurry back when he heard he was wanted, but that might take a day or more because the portly judge travelled only by stage.

Pete stared at his brother. The iron

bars seemed to emphasise the difference between them. He saw the mocking smile on Harry's lips, then his brother spoke:

'Well, this is it, Pete. I'm where you and pa think I ought to be. I'm the sinful man — the waster — the nogood — and now the murderer!'

Pete threw an angry glance back. 'You seem to think this is some sort of joke! Are you a fool, Harry? Why do you act like this? Why can't I get some sense out of you?

'I've heard all your explanations about Polly Bliss — and none of 'em make any sense! You just keep on sayin' that you didn't kill her! Hell, she was strangled — and you were found in the bedroom with her!'

'That sure was inconvenient,' murmured Harry Hadfield. His taunting smile seemed fixed as he stared back at Pete through the cell bars. 'It ain't decent bein' found in a bedroom with a young girl, dead or alive.'

'Go ahead — make fool talk all the

way to the gallows!' Pete swung away, sick at heart. Although few people realized it, he had always wished Harry would be a real brother, a sort of *companero*; but as they got older, leaving their teens behind, Harry had gone his wild way, avoiding work on the TT range. Heavy drinking, gambling and general lawlessness might be accepted to a point in a frontier town, but the murder of a pretty girl who'd been popular in the community, was something no man could get away with. And he would not get away with it. There was still talk of lynching and Sheriff Tom Sharkey was out of town. The situation was ugly.

Harry turned his head away as if tired. 'Go get a bed somewhere, brother of mine. You can't ride back to the ranch tonight. I'm plumb tuckered and you must be the same. At least I got me a bed . . .'

'I'd still like a sensible account of what happened in that bedroom with Polly Bliss,' Pete rasped out angrily, irritated by the stupid behaviour of his brother. He grasped the bars. 'For the last time, what really happened? Why did you grab her, strangle her?'

'Go away — get some shuteye. I figure you'll need it.'

'You were seen with the girl — bending over her — by old Ted Smith and his wife, Martha. They found you and Polly in the room she rented from 'em — and she was dead! You made off — went out through the window and then down the outside staircase.'

'Mighty handy, was that staircase,' Harry murmured. He shot a wicked glance at Pete. 'You know, Polly wasn't exactly the paragon of girlish virtue that most people in this town figured she was. You see, that staircase had been used before, lots of times.'

'That kind of talk will make you as popular as a colony of skunks in a church hall,' Pete warned. 'Why'd you run?'

'Seemed like certain galoots were shootin' off their mouths within five minutes of the alarm bein' raised — notably Mick Laverty. And Wally Bliss soon joined in. Wally never liked me, anyway. So I lit out. Seemed the best thing to do.'

'Like hell it was! It only made you appear guilty.'

'Sure. But I am guilty — everybody says so. You've heard 'em. Harry Hadfield strangled Polly Bliss in her bedroom, the low-down skunk! I heard more'n enough in the ten minutes before I hit the trail out of town. Men on the streets — two old women screechin' the news from one window to another — I figured it was better to ride out.'

'I wish I'd been in town to stop you.'

'Could've been you with Polly,' Harry said. 'But you never got around to her, did you? Nope, it was always Cilla with my upright brother! Cute little black-haired Cilla! I fancied her myself, but — '

'Leave her out of this. Cilla is as straight as they make 'em.'

'Sure — and too good for me, I guess. But Polly Bliss was some girl. But you wouldn't know, and there were only a few who did. It could've been almost anyone who killed her . . . she asked for it.'

Pete Hadfield slammed his right fist into his left palm. 'I'm sick of listening to your yap, Harry! I hope you talk more sense in front of Judge Harlan when he gets back if you last that long. Now, one more time — did you or didn't you kill that girl? If you didn't, why all this fool talk?'

'All right, I didn't kill her! And get to hell out of here! Does that make you happy!'

'That's still no explanation!' Pete Hadfield exploded. 'Give details, how it happened and why.'

'Pete, for God's sake, get away from here.'

A figure appeared in the narrow corridor outside the cells. Mick Laverty grinned nastily. 'You heard him, Hadfield — your brother wants you to get. I figure the same.'

'Sure seems like you itch to wear a badge again, Laverty,' rapped Pete. 'All right, I'm goin'. I take it Harry is safe here? When will the sheriff be back?'

'Tomorrow, I guess.'

'Too bad he hasn't got a real deputy . . . '

'I can do the job. I did it before.'

Pete stared into his eyes. 'I mean a man the sheriff can trust. You got kicked out of this office, if I remember right. You weren't the best deputy sheriff Perkinsville ever had by a long shot.'

'You Hadfields are all coyotes!' was Laverty's snarling reply. 'I don't like any one of you! And that goes for your pa — Gilbert Hadfield, the tricky old sidewinder. I sure heard some things about him.'

Sudden rage flared inside Pete. Most times he could control his temper, but Mick Laverty's insinuations were the last straw. Pete threw a short punch to the ex-deputy's jaw and sent him

28

reeling. Laverty's back slammed hard against the brick wall in the corridor. His mouth twisted and his lean young face glared hate as his hand flashed down to his gunbelt. But he didn't draw. The sudden hissing intake of his breath was as unpleasant as the expression on his face. 'Get, Hadfield! Get out of here! I'm doin' the deputy's job, badge or no badge! Your brother will stay behind them bars unless some jaspers figure otherwise!'

'He'd better be safe! I'm holdin' you responsible.'

Pete Hadfield decided there was nothing more he could do. It was not practical to ride back to the TT ranch just to inform his father of events; that would take him too far away from the scene. Opposite the sheriff's office was a small hotel; maybe he could get a room with a window overlooking the street. He needed a wash badly. And a hot meal. For two days he'd eaten in the saddle — dry bread, jerky and water. He felt empty. And he needed a chance to think things out, to reason his way through the strange behaviour and talk of his half-brother . . . because there was something odd about the death of Polly Bliss.

The brown mare and the black gelding were outside the law office. Pete walked them around to a livery where he found the ancient German hostler smoking an old curved pipe.

'Rub 'em down,' said Pete. 'Grain and water 'em. I'll see you in the mornin'.'

'Ja, you iss welcome . . . '

Pete Hadfield crossed the street to the hotel. Two blocks down, the saloon, Sal's Place, was lit up and noisy. At a T junction, a few hundred yards away and close to the cattle yards, lay another saloon, the Bonanza. Apart from a few solitary lights in other buildings and homes, this was the usual night-time scene in Perkinsville. It was not a large town; El Paso to the west was the real centre.

Ten minutes later he had his room on

the main street, and he spent some minutes looking down thoughtfully and grimly at the lighted sheriff's office below and on the other side of the street. A knock sounded on the door and a small old fellow staggered in with a big jug of hot water, some soap and a towel. Pete tipped the man, then he washed quickly but thoroughly. After that he went downstairs to an eating room in the little hotel. Someone was cooking in the back of the place and the small old fellow brought Pete the result — a hot sizzling steak with onions, rice and green peppers.

He was back in his room in a short time, staring down at the sheriff's office and the light. The street seemed quiet except for the noise emanating from Sal's Place. He wondered if he dared try to sleep. He needed rest, of course, but the fact was that he could do nothing for Harry until sunup. Even then he could only go around town asking a few discreet questions. Ted Smith and his wife, Martha, might have something to say. If Harry was safely locked away, the next moves were up to Sheriff Tom Sharkey and Judge Harlan when they hit town.

Pete Hadfield lay on the bed, half asleep and fully dressed, his gun heavy in its holster. Part of his brain was ready to register any noise or disturbance in the street below; the other part was drowsy. Half-formed dreams of the ride into the wastelands after his brother swirled like senseless images in his mind. Something was sucking him down into the realm of the unconscious.

A mile-deep sleep possessed him. He didn't hear the handle of the unlocked door softly turn, and he was unaware of the shadowy figure that crept into the room and paused over him.

The intruder had a gun that he turned in his hand. With a great degree of skill, as if he had done this trick before, he brought the shiny butt down on Pete's skull just once.

3

Lynch Mob!

The crowd from Sal's Place had spilled into the street. Sal, a huge woman with whom no one dared argue, had decided to close up for the night because tempers were flaring inside the saloon. Sal figured there might be some damage done before long and she was sick of paying for breakages. Also, no one was playing at the card tables and so profit was zero. So she got her shotgun and forced them all out throught the batwings. A few went home in a disgruntled mood, but most of them stayed in the street. With good cause . . .

Mick Laverty, assisted by Wally Bliss, repeatedly shouted to all and sundry, 'He killed Polly! Strangled her in her room, the dirty snake!'

And Wally joined in with, 'What sort of town is this! She could have been your sister or your wife. He raped her and then he killed her!'

'Harry Hadfield's a cocky bastard of a young hellion!' a man shouted drunkenly.

'I've had a bellyful of old man Hadfield!' snarled another. 'Beat me down in some deals!'

'It was rape!' screamed Wally again.

A man hitched at his gunbelt. 'I'd gun him down if it was my sister!'

'He killed her with his hands!' Mick Laverty grabbed a man's vest. 'You hear that? He strangled the poor kid!'

'Well, he'll hang,' muttered one man, over and over again. 'He'll hang for sure.'

'Legal hangin' is too good for the skunk!' Mick Laverty bawled. He jumped to the edge of a water trough and managed to balance his boots on the two sides. 'Listen! Listen! We're the law in town right now! So I say we should hang the dirty killer . . . hang him!'

There were a few men in the crowd who appeared to be dubious, but they remained silent. Attracted by the row, some men left the Bonanza and joined the mob. Some were out-of-town range hands and a few were strangers, but most of them had their homes in Perkinsville and had known the dead girl. With drink in them, their indignation increased, with Mick Laverty's howling harangue pushing them on.

'Sure, let's get that girl-killer!'

'Go get a rope and a buggy!'

While Pete Hadfield lay unconscious, unable to hear anything, the enraged men surged towards the sheriff's office. Mick Laverty dropped back — he didn't want to play a leading part in the actual lynching for fear of future reprisals. He had brought the crowd to a high pitch of anger with drink the main ingredient of the unholy brew he'd stirred.

The door of the office was open — Laverty had seen to that — and the key to Harry Hadfield's cell lay in plain view on the desk. Men stamped in heavily, glaring angrily at the white-faced man behind the bars. Then the cell was unlocked and Harry Hadfield was dragged out. His protests were futile against the uproar.

Two men had secured a four-wheeled buggy and a swiftly harnessed horse. Rope was found and a man fashioned a noose. On a corner lot was a large cottonwood which had been the local hanging tree since Perkinsville was a mere handful of shacks, but no man had died on a rope for more than ten years. The last executed man had been a Mexican cut-throat who left no mourners.

The angry crowd rushed to the hanging tree and the rope was thrown over a branch, then the buggy was wheeled beneath the limb and Harry Hadfield was pushed along by four enraged men.

'You blasted skunk! Kill a girl, would you?'

'Sure was a pretty kid — never done

no wrong to no one! Strangled, by God!'

'Lemme beat the hell outa him!'

The furious exclamations ripped through the night air. By this time each man felt that the lynch party was just retribution for a man who had killed a popular, pretty young girl. To them the hangnoose was a symbol of justice and no law was needed to enforce it.

As Harry Hadfield was lifted on to the bed of the buggy, a tall man rode a spirited horse into town and reined up grimly in the shadows. One glance and he read the scene. But it was something he hadn't expected. A lynching! He couldn't allow it to happen. Whatever the consequences, he had to do something.

He was glad now that he had flung on nondescript clothes for the night ride. He could be almost anybody in this frontier town. If he covered his face, he wouldn't be recognized.

It was the work of only seconds to loosen the bandanna from around his neck and then tie it firmly across the lower part of his face, leaving only his eyes visible, and they were shaded when he pulled the black hat firmly down on his brow.

He pulled the Winchester from the saddle scabbard and checked the action. He would have to ride the horse in and make his play. It couldn't be delayed any longer.

The mob was ready to put the noose around Harry Hadfield's neck.

The big man urged his horse forward, came to the perimeter of the crowd and brought the rifle stock to his shoulder.

'Hold it!' he shouted. 'I'll drill the first man who makes a fool play! Get him down off that buggy — pronto!'

He'd disguised his voice, made it harsh and low, an ugly rasp.

'Cut the bindings on his wrists!' He swung the rifle over the gaping crowd, aware of the astonished silence. He knew he couldn't hold them off for long. He had to push everything in one quick play.

'Who the hell are you, mister?' one man asked.

The tall man sighted along the Winchester and the long barrel arced and then stopped on the man standing on the buggy beside Harry Hadfield. 'I said cut the damn bindings!'

Fear hit the man and he brought out a small folding pocketknife from a trousers pocket. He cut the three turns of rope around Harry Hadfield's hands. Harry jumped to the edge of the buggy, his gaze flicking over the mob and on to the lone rider.

'Get up behind me,' ordered the man with the Winchester huskily.

Harry Hadfield wondered who was behind the bandanna mask. The voice puzzled him for a moment, then he exclaimed, 'God, no!' But it was a muttered sound that no other man heard.

He knew he had to act speedily, while the mob was under the spell of the pointed Winchester. He raced through the lynch mob as they parted. He reached the horse and vaulted up behind the masked rider. Only then did he know for sure that his first suspicions were correct. Only seconds had elapsed since the big man had levelled the long, new Winchester. Now the horse was viciously rowelled into a fast gallop.

Mick Laverty was the first to react. 'Get them! Gun them down, damn it! Don't let 'em get away!'

Laverty drew his Colt and triggered wildly at the galloping horse. It was crazy shooting, stimulated by hatred and anger. The fact that he had been cowed into submission by the appearance of one man infuriated him.

Mick Laverty's shots were a signal for the other men to fire their guns. But it was just so much wasted lead. And they were still shooting after the big horse had turned the corner with its two riders.

Big Ben Link had left his home on the outskirts of town at the sound of the angry voices. On foot, it had taken him a long while to reach the scene of the attempted lynching, and he was in time only to see the two men on the galloping horse before they disappeared around the side of a building.

'What the hell goes on?' Link roared. He saw Mick Laverty and Wally Bliss racing down the street. Although he was twenty years older than these two, he sprinted after them. They halted to level handguns at the street corner, then fired at the distant target. Big Ben Link lunged up and bumped into them, spoiling their aim.

'Who started this lynch party?' he demanded. 'Was it you, Laverty? You're responsible for Harry Hadfield — you had the damn jail keys — '

'Wasn't me,' Laverty lied. 'The galoots in the saloon just got the idea on their own. They stormed in and hauled him out of the cell. You didn't expect me to stop 'em, did you?'

'You sure do hate that man!' said the angry Link. 'You wanted to see him danglin'! Is it because you fancied Polly Bliss?'

'He's a dirty, murderin' rat, that's all he is!'

'Murder ain't proved yet!' Ben Link pointed out. 'Now who the blazes was that galoot who rode off with Harry Hadfield? Does anybody know? Did anybody recognize him?'

'Some outlaw pal of his,' Wally Bliss snarled. 'When you bumped into us, you were protectin' a killer! Wait until the sheriff hears about this!'

'Wait till he hears about the attempted lynch party,' Ben Link said. 'He don't like that kind of thing and he'll be askin' you two some questions.'

'I ain't worried about that,' Mick Laverty clipped out. He turned, thrusting his gun into leather. 'Hadfield killed that girl and that's for sure. He was found with Polly's body — ain't that proof?'

'Well, it doesn't look good for Hadfield,' agreed Big Ben Link. 'But I won't be happy until there's been an investigation and time has been given to hear all stories and get the facts.'

'Ah, the hell with you, Ben Link! That killer got clear away and he's headin' for the dark trails. With his head start we could never find him in this darkness. Which means we rode them damned canyons for nothin'! Wally, are you comin'?'

The two men turned away, walked back and mingled with the arguing men in the street near the hanging tree. For some fifteen minutes the men stood in groups, talking and gesticulating, then some drifted home or strolled to the still-open saloon, the Bonanza.

★　★　★

Up in his hotel room Pete Hadfield stirred, rolled his head on the pillow and groaned. He blinked a few moments later and winced as lamplight lanced through his optic nerves. Eventually he sat up and felt at his head. His fingers touched dried blood. He had no idea why his head ached or why there had been bleeding. Then, slowly, he remembered going up to the hotel room and lying down.

Everything flashed back. Harry was in the jail across the street. He had to watch that jail; anything could happen.

He swung his feet off the bed and on to the floor, then he staggered to the window and stared down. He saw a group of five men standing outside the sheriff's office and recognized one as Big Ben Link. He felt at his head again and winced. Someone must have slugged him as he slept.

Something was wrong down there. Without any further delay he lurched along the hotel corridor and then went down the stairs and into the street. A man raised a shout as Pete stumbled towards the sheriff's office and the five men who stood there.

'There's the brother, by thunder! Maybe he was the masked man who busted up the lynch party!'

'How could it be him?' Ben Link

said. 'He can't be here and ridin' into the night at the same time!'

'He could have jumped off that horse and then came back into town!' A voice loaded with sneering hatred added to the idea put forward by the first man, and Pete recognised Mick Laverty in the small group for the first time. 'A neat trick, by hell! Yeah, that's it, men! He pulled that trick and he's got the goddamned nerve to walk back here. Ain't that just like a mangey Hadfield!'

Pete walked right up to Laverty and glared at him. 'What the hell are you talkin' about? Big Ben . . . ' he swung around to face the blacksmith ' . . . what goes on? What's this about Harry and a lynch party?'

'Where've you been?' asked Link grimly.

'I took a room in the hotel over there.'

'You ain't heard the all-fired row that's been goin' on? They were all set to lynch your brother.'

'I didn't hear a damn thing,' Pete rasped, 'because some louse came into my room and rapped me on the head. I've been out cold, I guess. Is Harry safe?'

'He is,' Link said. 'Some smart *hombre* held a rifle on the lynch party and got your brother away.'

Pete Hadfield expelled his breath slowly and looked around. 'Now who would pull a trick like that?'

'You would! You could've been that rannigan!' returned Laverty. 'You're about the same size.'

'I've got a bump on my head that proves my story,' Pete snapped. 'Take a look, Big Ben.' And Pete inclined his dark head to show the bruise. 'Somebody wanted me to have a long sleep — and he knew where to find me! Maybe his idea was to keep me quiet while the lynch mob was organized. Seems to me there's only two snakes that are really interested in seein' Harry swing — and that's Wally Bliss and you, Mick Laverty! Maybe one of you slugged me in that hotel room . . . '

'You're loco!' Laverty clipped out.

'Yeah? Well, you were rantin' on about seein' Harry swing all the way back to town. You sure hate him enough for the lynchin' to be your idea. With me temporarily out of the way, you had no opposition.'

'I say you're crazy!'

'What went on with you and Polly Bliss?' Pete stepped close to the ex-deputy and grabbed his vest. 'Why the big hate? Did she tell you to get lost? I know she sent you packin' one night at the church dance . . .'

'You hear everything, don't you, Hadfield!' Mick Laverty sneered. 'Well, you won't be able to help your half-brother much longer! His name'll be on a Wanted dodger pretty soon — wanted for murder! He won't find any-place to hide. Not even stinkin' outlaws can stomach no-good girl killers!'

'You seem too damn certain that Harry did it,' Pete said. 'How do you know how the girl died? There's been no investigation so far that's worth a busted cent!'

'I just know he strangled her!' Laverty tried to pull free of Pete's grip.

'I'm pretty certain you handed me that wallop on the head,' Pete raged. 'So put up your hands and fight, Laverty! Let's see if you're as good with your fists as you are with your tongue!'

It was a fight that Mick Laverty couldn't back away from. Pete Hadfield raised his fists in a prizefighter stance, then he stepped in and rammed out a piston-like left. It connected and rocked the other man. Seething with rage, Mick Laverty retaliated.

Pete was at a disadvantage. He had a sore head for a start, and the events on the trail had sapped most of his strength. In truth he wasn't the kind of man who indulged in brawling. But he was convinced that Laverty had slugged him — and this was enough to infuriate any man.

Pete ripped a left hook to Laverty's chin and sent him reeling back. Laverty had rough-housed in his time, but only when he had the edge on his opponent.

He tried to fling a blow at Pete, but the young man side-stepped smartly and Laverty over-balanced. Pete clipped him on the ear, a blow that stunned the ex-deputy and made his guard drop.

Laverty knew that an orthodox fight wasn't for him. Pete Hadfield was too good at fisticuffs. So he suddenly kicked out. His boot caught Pete in the stomach and doubled him over. Laverty grinned, circled and tried the trick again as the others looked on grimly. Laverty's boot went out and caught Pete on the shin. Pete stumbled and fell, putting out a hand to support himself.

Mick Laverty whipped out his gun, twisted the Colt around in his hand and advanced, butt raised. 'By hell, I'll spill his brains in the dust! Should've done it the first time . . . '

As the gunbutt was brought down, Ben Link rammed out an iron-hard arm to knock the weapon to the side. A lifetime of hammering at his forge had made Ben one of the toughest men in town. Laverty's gunbutt arced through empty air.

Pete Hadfield jumped to his feet and moved in again, fists ramming out unmercifully. He caught Mick Laverty on the jaw with a hard right and the man fell to the dusty road and lay there, momentarily senseless.

Pete staggered, his stomach turning. He felt ready to drop as he turned to Ben Link. 'You helped me there, Ben — thanks.'

'I think you were right about him sluggin' you,' the blacksmith said, then he and the other men watched as Mick Laverty sat up slowly and glared around. Sighting Pete Hadfield, he muttered thickly:

'I'm gonna kill you some day. You better start lookin' over your shoulder, feller . . . '

Pete Hadfield turned his back on Laverty and returned to the hotel, where he had dumped his saddle-bags. He stood at the window looking down at the street and wondering if there was any lead he could follow, but he decided it was too late to do anything effective.

Who had helped Harry escape? It seemed that no one had been able to identify the rider. He had carried a Winchester, but that in itself wasn't unusual.

Pete racked his brains wondering who had effected the rescue. And why should the man mask his face? Obviously, he wasn't a wanted outlaw.

There were no answers to Pete's questions. And there was nothing else he could do at this time of night. The streets were quiet except for some hard drinkers still keeping the Bonanza open — he could hear their distant laughing and shouting — and there was no sheriff or judge with whom to confer. He wanted to question Ted and Martha Smith, but that would have to wait until morning. He also wanted to see Cilla, but that, too, would have to be held off. He would ride out to the ranch and see his father, but he decided that the ten-mile ride would have to wait as well.

Pete turned the big iron key in the room door, then he placed the back of a chair under the handle and lay down, his gun within reach on another chair near the bed. He was tired and muscle weary and his mind was too full of whirling images for sleep. The bruise on his head was sore. But he lay resting and, eventually, sleep overtook him.

★ ★ ★

The next day, after a quick breakfast, he went to the sheriff's office where he found Mick Laverty talking to two men. The unofficial deputy was keen to organise a posse and go after Harry. Pete listened grimly for some minutes, but offered no comment. Then he turned to leave the scene and found himself face to face with Wally Bliss. The small man stared hard at Pete and then brushed past him and entered the office.

Some minutes later Pete got his black from the livery. He paid the hostler, saddled the animal, looked it over and decided that the last two days of riding hadn't damaged the gelding to any extent. He stepped up into the saddle and walked the black down the main stem, noting the freight wagons being loaded, the stage taking on passengers, sounds from the blacksmith's forge. He figured he'd talk to Ted Smith and his wife. He wanted to hear their account of the finding of Polly's body.

Now, quite suddenly, he remembered how Harry had shouted at him, 'I'll say it loud and clear — just for the hell of it — I didn't kill Polly Bliss!'

Was Harry lying? If not, why didn't he back his statement with facts? It wasn't good enough just to say he hadn't killed her. It was, by Harry's own admission, a fact that Ted Smith and Martha had found him crouching over the girl's body . . .

The big frame house on Santa Street had an upper floor. There was a wooden staircase at the back, leading to a balcony. The house was big, too big for the old couple, and they had often taken in boarders. Pete Hadfield tied the big black to the hitching rail outside, went up a few steps and knocked on the door.

In the sitting room, where old china stood on a big black dresser, Martha Smith asked Pete to take a chair. 'Ted will be down in a moment. These days he sleeps in a bit, what with his bad back and all . . . '

'I'd like to talk about Polly Bliss,' began Pete.

Martha Smith's face clouded. 'A terrible affair . . . poor girl . . . '

'Can I see her room?'

'I don't mind, Mr Hadfield. But I can't see what good all this will do . . . '

'I've got to start checkin' out Harry's story somewhere,' said Pete grimly. 'The sheriff's away — maybe he'll be back today and maybe he won't.'

'Your brother — I — I — don't know what to think,' the old lady said falteringly. She was tall and erect, with a pale face and grey hair. Pete had heard she was about seventy years old.

Mrs Smith led the way up the stairs and on the landing they met Ted Smith. He was a year or two older than his wife and not as fit. He wore black pants and a collarless flannel shirt. It seemed he had just left his bed. He blinked watery blue eyes at Pete Hadfield.

'You! Goshdarn it — your brother — it ain't right — we had that poor dead girl in this house, and now you come nosin' around!'

'Now, Ted, Mr Hadfield just wants to ask some questions,' said Martha. 'And look at the bedroom . . . '

'That girl!' grumbled the old man. 'We should never have had her in the house. I told you that more'n once, Martha.'

'Hush! Don't talk like that of the dead.'

Pete felt sympathy for the old couple. He didn't like disturbing them but there were vital issues at stake.

'Why shouldn't you have had her in the house, Mr Smith?' Pete asked.

'She was no good!' the old man flared. 'We knew all about that staircase!'

'Ted! Poor Polly was — '

'She sure had her share of galoots chasin' her!' Ted Smith was incensed. 'If you ask me, she got what was comin' to her! Oh, I heard plenty some nights when I couldn't sleep!'

'Ted, you never said this before . . . '

'But I did! You just didn't want to listen, Martha.'

'Who visited Polly Bliss late at night in that room?' Pete put the question directly to the old man. 'It's important, Ted. I've got to know.'

'Well, I saw a lot of 'em. They came creepin' down that damn staircase. But I guess it's no use blamin' any of 'em. I was a young buck myself once.'

'Ted!'

'I saw three different *hombres*,' said Ted Smith quietly. 'One was your brother, Harry. Then there was an oldish galoot who I never saw properly yet. But I sure saw that hellion jasper who was a deputy once . . . Laverty. Don't know why he bothered to come at all! All they did was argue. I heard her yell for him to get to hell out of her room more'n once. Huh! She sure was no lady, that one!'

4

Laverty — Drygulcher

Pete Hadfield rode the black steadily across the rolling hills, skirting the wire fences of homesteads near the town. He had left the trail that ran through the Pecos Valley to El Paso in the far west and taken the rougher but more direct route to the TT range. The fertile land near the springs around Perkinsville had been taken over by homesteaders. The TT range started ten miles out. Here the grass was sparse, often brown in summer but nourishing enough for the rangy cattle that moved incessantly across it. The TT outfit was fairly big in land area, but the herds were modest. The beef was trail-driven to Alpine and from there it went by rail to San Antonio.

Pete was on his way to see his father;

he had to tell him about the events connected with Harry.

Pete Hadfield saw the little burro breast a rim and pick his way down the grass- and cholla-studded slope. The oldster was perched stiffly on the animal's back.

Pete rode up. 'Are you still headin' for town, Jo-Jo?' The old man's grey whiskers seemed even thicker this day. His surprisingly clear blue eyes squinted in his weatherbeaten face. He grinned at Pete, showing discoloured teeth with black gaps.

'Say, I been to see your old man! Didn't make it to town. I spent the night at the ranch.'

'You did? What sort of yarn did you spin to my pa? He usually runs saddlebums off his range.'

'Saddlebum!' Jo-Jo looked hurt. 'Now that ain't no way to talk to me!'

'Sorry, pardner, but that's the way my pa sees unemployed people. And he's got a lot of temper.'

'I sure found that out,' Joe Johanson

said a bit ruefully. 'At first, I mean. He didn't even want to pass the time of day with me — but then I told him about how I met you and your brother . . . '

'What did he say?'

'He was plenty agitated, I guess. I had to tell him how them galoots from town cornered your brother Harry and how the whole parcel of you headed back to Perkinsville for the night.'

'Was pa worried?'

'Well, he kind of glowered into that big rock fireplace in your ranch house. Then he told me to get some chow from the cook and to bed down in the bunkhouse.' Jo-Jo's eyes brightened. 'Sure was a nice change for an old jasper like me!'

'Guess it was after desert livin'. Well, *adios*, oldtimer.' Pete Hadfield urged the black up the slope and down the other side, then he rode at a fast walk along a rocky draw. Deep in thought, he was unaware of his surroundings. So his father knew that Harry had been caught. But he would know nothing

60

about the attempted lynching and the escape, so there was at least that much to talk about.

Pete approached the old Comanche War Rocks. These yellow sandstone buttes rose abruptly from the semi-arid land, six of them in a line, standing like sentinels. The old warring Indians had made carvings on the sides of the rocks as they travelled between Mexico and their northern homes, and they'd had a lot of superstitious respect for the wind- and rain-corroded buttes.

But at that moment Pete Hadfield wasn't giving much attention to the old rocks — until the rifle cracked from their cover. The slug thudded into the ribcage of the big black gelding.

The animal reared in pain and sudden terror. Pete kept his balance in the saddle by sheer instinct and horsemanship. But then the black's forelegs plunged back to earth and buckled. Pete was flung from the saddle as the horse rolled over, kicking in agony.

Pete Hadfield was a rancher's son and had worked mainly on the range, but he knew the tricks of preservation in a hard land.

He rolled behind the gelding as the animal died in pain, eyes rolling and nostrils flaring. Pete's gaze swept over the Comanche War Rocks ... but which one was providing the rifleman with cover? A fusillade of shots sounded and bullets slammed into the dusty ground around the prone horse. A few slugs rammed into the still body of the unfortunate gelding.

Pete Hadfield lay absolutely flat, then his gaze travelled fast to his right where a huge boulder sat on the flat ground. The rock was solid cover but maybe it was a case of exchanging the frying pan for the fire.

There was silence from the buttes; no target, nothing at which to throw a desperate shot. There was only one thing he was sure about; his unknown attacker was a bad shot.

Pete Hadfield reached for his rifle in

the saddle scabbard. He had to pull hard to get the gun out because the body of the gelding was lying on it. As the rifle moved out inch by inch, he kept his eyes on the buttes. A few more tugs and the rifle was clear. While he checked the action the man behind the cover of the buttes decided to pump off some more wild shots. The slugs spat into the earth all around the dead horse.

'You're sure one poor hand with a rifle, *amigo*,' Pete muttered. 'Now who the blazes are you? Do I know any bad-eyed rannigan who'd like me dead?'

With the instinct that sometimes comes clearly in such a situation, he knew that the rifleman was Mick Laverty. The man had said, 'I'm gonna kill you some day. Start lookin' over your shoulder.'

Was the ex-deputy such a lousy shot? Probing his memories of the man from the little he knew about his days as a badge-toter, he began to recall some of the things he'd heard about Mick Laverty.

'Sure,' somebody had once said, 'that galoot couldn't hit a barn door at six paces.'

So Laverty had ridden out after him. He'd got ahead, probably riding in a concealing draw for some miles. Had Laverty been watching when he visited old Ted Smith and Martha? It was quite likely.

'So you want me dead . . . dry-gulched . . . ' Pete Hadfield mumbled. 'Guess you just hate all Hadfields . . . you certainly have it in for Harry — and now for me . . . '

That line of thought certainly tied in with Mick Laverty's attempt to hustle a lynch party into existence the other night.

Maybe Laverty was a rotten hand with a rifle, but it looked like the man had the edge on him. He had him pinned down with only a dead horse for cover.

Pete decided to let the drygulcher

know his identity was not a secret. 'Hey, Laverty, you ain't too good with that gun, are you? Do you hear me? I know who you are!'

Then Laverty's voice came back. 'I'm goin' to kill you, Hadfield. No man bests me in a fight!'

'That makes you a killer, Laverty!'

The man's snarling answer rasped across the silent wasteland. 'Your dirty brother killed that girl!'

'What was she to you, Laverty? I've been told you visited her room a number of times. You didn't always get a nice reception, it seems; in fact, you were heard arguin'!'

'Your dandy brother set her against me! I figured to court Polly Bliss but your stinkin' brother got in the way.'

'You sure kept those bedroom visits a secret!' shouted Pete. 'Were you ashamed of how she couldn't stand the sight of you?'

'The hell with you, Hadfield!' Laverty bellowed. 'You think what you like! Sure, Polly and me never met much in public — but she wanted me, all right! She just figured to keep me dancin' to her tune, that's all. Well, that was all right with me — but then Harry had to go and pester her!'

'The way I see it, you were the one who pestered her!'

'She liked me, you lyin' scum!'

Pete thought that if he riled the man enough he might show himself. The moment he presented himself as a target, no matter how slight, a slug would cut the air in his direction.

'Seems there were others who visited that room at the top of the staircase!' Pete taunted. 'It sure looks to me like Polly was a lady of easy virtue.'

'Damn you, Hadfield!'

'Maybe it was you who strangled the girl,' Pete flung out. 'Did it happen during one of your fights? Was that it?'

'You mangey polecat, you know damn well that Harry was caught with the girl — and she was dead! He done it!'

'Ain't been proved!'

'He'll hang — like the dirty no-account murderer he is!' Laverty screamed. 'Right now Wally Bliss and some men are out looking for the swine! After I've killed you, I'm gonna join up with 'em.'

Pete Hadfield stared grimly at the tall yellow buttes, wondering just where Mick Laverty was hiding. The age-old rocks brooded in the sun. The morning was wearing on and there were many things to do; he wanted to talk to his father about Harry, then he could ride over the trail to El Paso looking for the sign of his brother. But right now he was stranded. It was six miles to the TT outfit, and to get there he had to fight his way out of this trap. The buttes hid Laverty and his horse, as they had sheltered Indians when the marauding bands of Kiowas, Apaches and Comanches had come down these trails.

The silence grew heavier. Pete decided to push Laverty's reactions to the limit. He could take a calculated risk because of Laverty's limitations as a rifleman. So Pete gripped his

Winchester, went into a crouch, and then ran for the white boulder, boot toes digging into the dry earth. A second or two of time-lag demonstrated that Laverty had been surprised, and then the shots came. Dust spat up around Pete but the shots were badly placed and Pete kept sprinting for the solitary boulder. Finally he dived behind the cover of the sun-bleached rock as the last bullet dug into the earth yards behind. Pete sprang up again, figuring that Laverty had triggered off his last bullet. He would have to reload.

Pete raced like an attacking Indian, firing from the hip at the spot where he had noted the rifle flashes. He sprinted desperately for the rounded shape of the nearest butte. His rifle fire would, he hoped, pin down Laverty, even slow down the man's reloading. It was the only chance he had, unless he wanted to roast out there beside his dead horse for hours.

He made it to the yellow butte, his magazine empty, his mouth sucking at the dry air. He flattened against the rock and snicked shells from his ammunition belt that he rammed into the Winchester. When the next play started he'd give Mick Laverty a shock! Maybe one of them would end up as buzzard bait.

Rifle loaded, Pete stepped warily around the curving rock face. Unless the ex-deputy had moved his position, he would still be on the south side of the other butte.

All at once the sound of hoofs on loose shale came to Pete's ears. The clatter lasted only a few seconds and then Pete leaped out of cover. He saw Mick Laverty on a scraggy mustang. The man was getting out. Pete whipped up his rifle and fired. At that moment the horse's flying hoofs took Laverty around the curve of the butte.

Pete raced after the escaping drygulcher. He halted again when he had a clear view of the man and he fired off another shot. But the mustang's pounding hoofs had taken Laverty out of range.

Pete Hadfield lowered his gun grimly and looked around. The black gelding lay like a scab on the yellow earth. Well, Mick Laverty had given him a long, hot walk over terrain where only sidewinders and lizards lived.

Pete cursed the man. He took the saddle off the black, put it over his shoulder, and walked grimly away. If Mick Laverty had been even a fair marksman, Pete would be dead by now. It was a sober reflection.

For a mile or so Pete Hadfield trudged under the weight of the saddle. He wondered if he should ditch it in a cache of rocks and return later. After another mile he knew this was a good idea. He was taking punishment, for his high-heeled boots weren't designed for walking for any distance over this sort of land.

So Wally Bliss and an unofficial posse were out looking for sign of Harry's trail. And maybe Laverty would join them.

Pete cached the saddle and noted the

spot. Good saddle leather cost money; he'd pick it up as soon as possible. He walked on, cradling the rifle.

He'd trudged some four miles when he saw the distant rider coming along the rim above the valley. Pete, his eyes attuned to viewing over great distances, was pretty sure that he was looking at Sam Lacey, one of the TT's ranch-hands. He recognized the big, broad shoulders, the steeple-shaped hat. He whipped out his sixgun and fired two shots.

It was typical of Sam Lacey that he did not rush towards the distant speck that was a man. He reined in his horse and waited a few seconds, then he urged the mount forward at a walk. Pete shouted Lacey's full name and only then did the ranch hand rowel his animal into a gallop.

Minutes later Pete said, 'Am I glad to see you!' He grinned into the steady, inquiring eyes of the older man. 'One thing I know — a cow waddy sure hates walkin'. Gimme a hoist up . . . '

'What happened to your black, Pete?'

'Stone dead, Sam. Killed by a drygulcher by the name of Mick Laverty . . . '

'That galoot!' said Lacey slowly. 'But why?'

'Because he hates my guts and Harry's!' Pete hunched into position behind Sam and the big horse moved forward, haunches taking the double load easily. As they rode, Pete gave Sam a brief account of what had happened. Then he said, 'How's pa? He knows by now that Harry was taken back to the jail but he doesn't know he escaped from the lynchin' party. An old galoot named Jo-Jo called at the ranch last night to tell pa about Harry bein' arrested.'

'A lynching,' Sam Lacey murmured. 'That's bad . . . '

'You haven't said how pa is, Sam.'

'Can I talk honest? He's in a real bad temper — yes, sir! Guess it's gotta be about Harry. As for Jo-Jo, I saw that oldster last night in the bunkhouse, but

I didn't pay him much attention.'

'Seems he told pa about Harry bein' taken back to Perkinsville, but old Jo-Jo knew nothin' about the lynch party last night . . . '

The horse jogged on and Sam said, 'That girl was real bad medicine, Pete.'

'Did you know her?'

'Me? No . . . but I heard things . . . '

'How's that, Sam? You don't go to town very much.'

'Still, I hear things.'

Pete Hadfield frowned over these cryptic remarks and was silent for some moments before saying, 'Everybody figures it's a sure thing that Harry killed Polly. I ain't had much out of him that makes sense. First he says he didn't kill her and then he covers up with a lot of nonsense . . . fool talk . . . '

'You found him, huh?'

'I tracked him nearly to the border. He got careless.'

'Sure must be strange bringin' your own brother back for a trial.'

'Pa told me to get after him.' Pete

73

sighed. 'Harry just won't explain how come he was found with the dead girl.'

'I figure he didn't do it,' Sam said.

Pete Hadfield grasped Sam's arm. 'Do you know anythin' you should be tellin' me?'

'How can I know anythin'? Like you said, I don't hit town very much, me bein' a bit long in the tooth.'

'Hell, you're not that old, Sam. You should have married instead of making your home at the ranch.'

Pete Hadfield felt the other man's back stiffen. Then, 'I had enough of women. I think you know that.'

'Sorry, Sam. I guess I'm yappin' too much.'

The rest of the ride was conducted in a silence of Sam Lacey's choosing. He gave only grunts to Pete's few remarks and seemed to be consumed by inner thoughts. Pete couldn't see his face, but there was something in the ranch hand's attitude that puzzled him. When the buildings of the TT spread came into view he began to look forward to seeing his father again.

The big gate in the ranch yard fence bore the capitals, TT, carved on a big oak plaque. The corrals, barns and bunkhouse were set on the blank side of the ranch house, with a pair of old cottonwoods as spacers between the two groups of buildings. Behind the frame and brick house the land rose steeply to a huddle of yellow bluffs and white boulders. A spring bubbled generously from a rocky outcrop and formed a large pool in a smooth basin. That water supply had flowed winter and summer for as long as anyone could remember.

Gilbert Hadfield had arrived in the country as a young man and had immediately claimed his land. He'd built two ranch houses because the first one had been burned down by raiding Comanches in the days when they rode the Great Comanche War Trail. His first wife had died in that Indian attack, three months after Harry was born. A nurse had looked after the lusty child until Gilbert Hadfield decided to marry again.

The second wife had lived only long enough to bear Pete, falling victim to an epidemic of smallpox that swept the small settlement of Perkinsville. Gilbert Hadfield had become a grim man, easily angered, caring only for his sons. A number of nursemaids had looked after the children in their early days, and Gilbert Hadfield had refused to even consider marriage again. He knew several women in the growing township only ten miles from his range, but he treated them as playthings, using them to satisfy his sexual needs. After all, the rancher was a strong, virile man, and although he periodically visited the small church in Perkinsville, he didn't confuse piety with morals.

Pete found his father studying some papers on his big mahogany desk. A quill pen in a stand decorated one corner of the desk, and a steel-nibbed writing instrument stood in the other. A ledger was open and lay on a large blotter. Gilbert Hadfield rose at once and fixed sombre grey eyes on his son.

'Well?'

'That oldster — Jo-Jo — says he told you about Harry last night.'

'He did. Anything else?' Gilbert Hadfield's deep voice was in keeping with his big, wide shouldered body.

'They tried to lynch Harry last night . . . ' Pete gave his father the details in a clipped voice. Then, he said, 'You don't seem surprised.'

'Nothing that happens to your reckless half-brother surprises me,' Gilbert Hadfield said crisply.

'Men are out lookin' for him now. D'you figure I should ride out and see if I can trace him?'

'He could be nearly to Mexico by now,' rasped the rancher.

'Then he'll be a wanted man for the rest of his life,' said Pete. He walked slowly to the natural stone wall and leaned against it. 'You wanted me to get him back for trial, Pa. Have you changed your mind?'

'He can ride to hell!' was the snarling answer. 'Has that hellion ever done anything for me? Did he work on the ranch? Did he ever earn his keep since the day he figured he'd learnt enough at school! No! He thought I'd keep his pockets filled with money while he drank and gambled and fooled with girls!'

'Harry would have settled down sooner or later,' Pete said. 'We've been through all this before, Pa. I don't mind workin' . . . '

'That's not the point. I expected Harry to toe the line. He's your older brother and his mother . . . well, the blazes with that — it's all so long ago.'

'So you think we should just let him ride on,' Pete said. 'And what if they collar him? Right now Wally Bliss and Mick Laverty are out scourin' the country for him.'

'They won't get within hollerin' distance — '

'How do you know, Pa?'

'Harry's as wily as an Indian!'

'I caught up with him.'

'Yeah, but you've got a cussed streak of persistence. Maybe you're like me in some ways.'

Pete began to build a cigarette. 'Sheriff Tom Sharkey might be back today, or at least tomorrow — and he won't rest until wanted posters are in every damned law office from San Antonio to El Paso. Runnin' will just about prove Harry's guilt. He kept tellin' me he didn't kill the girl, then he'd talk a load of hogwash as if it was all a joke. I don't know what the hell to think.'

'Ridin' the owlhoot trail will suit him right down to the ground,' Gilbert Hadfield barked. 'He was side-kick to Duke Malden, as you know.'

'Seems to me that you've changed your mind, Pa, about having Harry stand trial. Why?'

'Because he's wild and free and that's the way he'll run, like some prairie-born stallion. Maybe it's just as well that way, Pete.'

Pete Hadfield lit his cigarette and looked down at his dusty clothes. He said, 'I think I'll get somethin' to eat and then have a bath.' He paused. 'I made some inquiries at Ted Smith's house. It seems that Polly Bliss was pretty free and easy.'

Gilbert Hadfield's bleak grey eyes flashed. 'Then she's small loss!'

'Other men figured in her life. She let them call late at night in her room. They got in by way of a back staircase . . .'

His father's face contorted in anger. 'I don't want to hear about that — that — damned hussy! You hear me, Pete?'

A quick temper was part of Gilbert Hadfield's character, but Pete was surprised at the sudden flare-up. Then he remembered Sam Lacey's words. 'He's in a real bad temper! Yes, sir!'

An hour later, fed, bathed and clad in clean brown pants and a checked shirt, Pete Hadfield walked to the western fence, climbed to the top rail and stared over the land to the bluish haze that was the Sacramento Mountains.

Smoking another cigarette, he stared into the heat-shimmered distance. He just couldn't leave the business of Harry and the dead girl as it was. Despite what his father thought, this wasn't the way to deal with the problem. Leaving Harry to ride the trail, one step ahead of the law, wanted for murder — no!

Pete flipped the cigarette butt away, slid down from the fence and walked back to the ranch house. The sounds around him didn't register. The distant bawling of cattle, sounding across the great valley for over a mile, the ring of a three-pound hammer on the anvil, the clatter as the cook came out of the bunkhouse with metal plates in a bucket — all these were background sounds of his environment and were all too familiar.

He was going after Harry, and he'd get the truth about Polly. He'd find Harry even if it meant crossing the border below El Paso. There was little doubt in Pete's mind that Harry would head for Mexico.

As Pete went through the ranch house, his father glanced at him.

'Have you got somethin' on your mind, Pete?'

'Yep. I've just got to talk to Harry again.'

'Thought so.' Gilbert Hadfield went to a window. 'You aim to ride out today?'

'Time-wastin' ain't one of my faults, Pa. Yes, I'll just get me a good horse from the stock, then — '

'Don't go, son!' Gilbert Hadfield turned, his face set hard.

Pete's eyes narrowed in surprise. 'You've sure changed your mind! Why shouldn't I go?'

'Harry won't thank you for pokin' your nose in.'

Pete shook his head. 'I've just got to talk to him, Pa!'

'I don't want you runnin' into grief. You told me that Laverty tried to kill you. Well, I don't want to lose two sons . . .'

'You haven't lost one yet, Pa. I'm gonna get right to the bottom of this thing. I'd like to know how Harry is travellin'. Who gave him a horse?'

'Must've been the man who rescued him from the lynch mob. I'm tryin' to figure out who that *hombre* might be. Maybe some friend of his in town?'

'Could have been a lot of men. He was masked. Maybe they doubled back to town and got a horse for Harry . . .'

Gilbert Hadfield turned to the window again and stared out grimly, a big-boned, sombre man who seemed to get little pleasure from life.

'I'm goin',' Pete said.

$\star$ $\star$ $\star$

The midday sun was burning down as Pete rode from the TT range and headed west. Somewhere in this wide, sparsely populated territory, Harry Hadfield was travelling. El Paso was a hundred miles off. There were three small towns on the way — Kinton,

Ramsy and Santa Arena. If Harry had gone through these little settlements, he may have been noticed, and a few questions would soon track him down. The trip to El Paso would take about three days in this hostile land. Pete would have to give the horse all due consideration. Hell-fire riding could be fatal to man and beast. Characteristically, Pete Hadfield knew it was the patient man who survived and the fool who succumbed.

5

Bully With a Badge

During two full days of slow, plodding riding Pete went through two of the small settlements where he stopped to talk with a few of the locals. At Kinton, the first place, a man answering to Harry's description had passed through. An oldster, occupying a rocking-chair on a porch, had seen Harry. Kinton was just five shacks in a rocky valley where some sheep were herded and a little gold was panned out of a stream. Here no man could move in or out without being seen. Ramsy was another settlement with hardly any reason for human habitation. Set on a hillside, it was more of a hideout for lawless rannigans than a town, and Pete Hadfield asked questions with one hand near his holster. Once again he learned that Harry had been here. And he had been riding a blown horse.

Pete wasn't surprised about the badly treated horse. Harry would push hard and to hell with the consequences. Pete walked his horse into Santa Arena at the tail end of the second day. He looked the place over. With the border only thirty miles away, the Spanish influence was strong here. A white adobe cantina flanked one side of the plaza and a mission with a tall bell-tower lent dignity to the other side. Santa Arena seemed to be a town of sheepherders and mule trains. On the hills around the area, grass grew well, with silvery cholla cacti studding the flat land along with sage and other desert growth. A man with capital was mining silver; the workings stood out on a hillside. Pete Hadfield had never been in the town before. He passed a dilapidated frame building which bore the faded sign: SHERIFF. But he didn't want the law, only evidence that he was on Harry's trail.

He got the evidence almost immediately when he saw the horse standing inside a livery barn. He thought there was something familiar about the horse, so he drew up his own mount, slid down from the saddle and entered the livery. He looked at the big haunches of the animal and saw the brand — TT.

Harry! There was no doubt. But how the devil did he get a TT stock animal? Had he cut back to the ranch that night and stolen the animal? If so, why hadn't anyone reported a missing horse?

Pete walked out of the livery, halted and then squinted down the sun-filled street. Some Mexican kids were playing in the dust. A big man, white and obviously a Texan, came out of the cantina, wiped his mouth and stared at Pete. A badge glinted on his shirt pocket.

Pete looked his own horse over. He hadn't pushed the animal and it was still fit. He'd watered his mount adequately and had let it graze. Maybe it needed a feed of oats right now, but it was certainly in better shape than the big horse in the livery. Harry, it seemed, from the state of his horse, had arrived in town hours ago. Why hadn't he pushed on to El Paso and the border?

The big man with the badge was still staring at him. It was a bold, insolent look and Pete didn't like it. The lawman hooked his thumbs in his gunbelt and settled down into a slow all-over appraisal of Pete. The process was unnecessarily long and offensive.

With a faint smile, Pete Hadfield led his horse into the shadowy interior of the livery. If Harry was in town, he could afford to rest the animal. There was no hurry. Time was on the side of the man who played things cool.

He found the liveryman, a lean young fellow with a mournful face. 'Will you feed my horse and rub it down?' Pete asked. 'What's the charge?'

'The usual.' The man tried to grin and only managed to look sorrowful. Pete unbuckled the cinch and slid the saddle off. He dumped the leather in a corner of the livery, got his saddlebags and rifle and made to move away. He'd find a hotel and then he'd seek out Harry. The cantina would be the first call.

'By the way,' Pete said to the liveryman, 'that big horse . . . I think I know the owner. When did he get into town?'

'First thing today, *amigo*. Just after sunup. Must've been travellin' long and hard 'cause that animal looked mighty tired. Big-boned horse, too . . . '

'Yeah. Do you know where the feller is right now? At the hotel maybe?'

The liveryman broke into a braying laugh but his face looked as though he was crying. 'That's sure good! Well, if that don't beat all . . . '

'What's so funny?'

'Hotel!' He kept laughing.

Pete grinned faintly. 'How about sharin' the joke?'

'Well, seems the joke is on that feller you asked about. Heads for the cantina first thing and there ain't nobody there except two rannigans from out of town. Guess the feller you knew took in one drink too many. Tequila, I guess. Should've used more salt with it . . . '

'What the devil are you gettin' at?'

'Well, he picks a fight with the other two galoots. One ends up at the vet with a slug in his leg and the other hardcase hightails it out of town.'

'What about the feller I know? Where is he?'

'He ain't in no hotel, that's for sure.' The liveryman chuckled. 'Right now he's in the calaboose — the sheriff here don't like trouble-makers!'

His face going hard suddenly, Pete Hadfield walked from the livery, carrying his saddle-bags and rifle. Suddenly he halted, deep in thought. When he looked up, the sheriff of Santa Arena was standing across the road, watching him suspiciously.

Pete had had enough of this treatment. He stared right back. The lawman's bold eyes met Pete's deliberate gaze, then the sheriff walked forward, his heavy boots making the boards creak. His attitude was that of a bully, a man who enjoyed exercising his authority. Pete waited calmly, his smile faintly contemptuous.

'You remind me of the jasper I got in a cell,' the sheriff said abruptly. The sneer in his voice added to the menace of his bulky presence.

'You got some galoot in jail?' Pete asked.

'Your spitting image almost, *hombre*.'

'Well, that's real nice. As long as it ain't me, Sheriff, I don't give a damn. Why tell me about it?'

'To begin with, the two of you rode in with horses wearin' the same brand.'

'Is that so?' Pete said easily. 'I bought this animal in Perkinsville. D'you know the place?'

'Don't hand me a load of bulldust, feller. I don't stand for any saddletramp tryin' to make a fool outa me. I'm Sheriff Chet Lancer and I boss this lousy town.'

'So it would seem,' said Pete mildly. 'Well, nice meetin' you, Sheriff. I've got to find me a hotel and a bite to eat.'

The lawman put a large spade-like hand before Pete's face. 'What brings you here to Santa Arena?'

'I'm on my way to El Paso.'

'You're handin' me some bulldust again. You've trailed in after that other galoot and I want to know why.'

Pete Hadfield held his grin. 'I think you're jumpin' to conclusions, Sheriff. I don't know a damn thing about this man.'

'Yeah? Well, he's gonna stink in jail until I figure he's had enough. I don't like ornery cusses. I do all the hellin' around in this town. I got it tied up. You either like me or you hate me. So I'll find out why you rode in and who the hell that other *hombre* is. I'll also learn why you both got horseflesh with the same brand. I will, mister, so just get used to the idea.'

Pete Hadfield had the impression that he was being allowed to walk away like a small boy who'd been properly chastised. It left a sour taste in his mouth. He didn't like the sheriff of Santa Arena one bit. The lawman was a real hardcase. If he found out that Harry was wanted for the murder of a pretty girl, that would be it. Of course, Wanted posters had not been circulated yet, but Sheriff Tom Sharkey would be back in Perkinsville by now and he would waste no time in asking the Federal Marshal to issue a description to all law officers. So Pete had to get Harry out of Santa Arena fast. Somehow.

Pete considered the situation as he walked into the hotel. He interrupted his thoughts long enough to get a room from the elderly Mexican desk clerk. Staring into the street from the window, he knew he had to approach the sheriff again and somehow get Harry released. In this wild land a shooting fracas didn't call for more than a day in jail and a fine.

If he could get Harry free, there would be time to talk, time to get to the real core of the puzzle: had Harry killed Polly Bliss?

Pete decided he could make a better impression on the lawman when he was washed and shaved and had some food inside him. He washed up first, then he shaved with his long-handled razor, using the warm water that was brought up to him. Then he changed into a clean shirt and trousers from his saddle-bags and beat the dust from his hat.

Finally he slicked his dark hair down with water and combed it. Tightening his gunbelt, he eased the .45 in and out of the holster. It was free and easy. He left the hotel and went to an eating house where he was served by a none-too-clean Mexican in a smudged apron.

He went down the boardwalk to the sheriff's office as the sun was setting behind the black-blue silhouette of the Sacramento Mountains. Maintaining a grim show of confidence, Pete entered the building, taking in at one sweep — the layout: the desk, the gun case, the door leading to the cell passage. Sheriff Chet Lancer stopped writing a letter to look up at Pete. Without his hat on, the sheriff's face seemed even more insolent. He had reddish hair and a bulbous nose. He was about forty, Pete thought.

'You again, feller!' The lawman's greeting was a taunt.

'Can I talk to you?'

'What about?'

'The man you have in the cell . . . '

'I got two right now. Which one do you want?' The man was sneering at him.

'The feller you say looks like me. Can I talk to him?' The sheriff gave a shake of his head.

'Nope.'

Pete took a deep breath. 'All right, Sheriff. Can I pay his fine? Tell me how much. I want him out. You're right about us lookin' alike. Fact is, he's a relative of mine and we got some business to do together in El Paso. I was to meet him there. So how about it?'

The sheriff looked up, enjoyment creasing his face. 'Now we're gettin' somewhere, *hombre*. I knew you were after him — the brand marks on the horses, the look about you and the way you went into that livery. Yeah. Well, now, let me see . . . '

'It was just a fight he got into, I understand.'

'You don't say! Just a fight, eh? Disturbin' the peace, shootin' a man — '

'A leg wound.'

'You been makin' inquiries?' sneered the other. 'What's the name of this hellion relative of yours? He won't tell me. I ought to bust him for that, refusin' to answer a lawman.'

'He's Ed Brown. I'm his cousin.'

Sheriff Chet Lancer got up. His movements were ponderous, heavy. He wouldn't be fast in a fight. But he was rough; even the way he pushed his chair back proved that. Pete had to lie to the man; he certainly wasn't going to mention the name Hadfield.

The big sheriff was grinning unpleasantly. As he watched Pete he took out his makings and rolled a cigarette. He lit the cigarette with a big sulphur match and then blew smoke at the young man.

'Sure, you can pay the fine, seein' you're so goddamn anxious to get him out of here. It costs money to feed prisoners.'

'How much?' Pete asked.

'Two hundred dollars.'

Pete Hadfield stared at the lawman in amazement. 'Why, that's plumb crazy! Two hundred! You wouldn't be gettin' more than forty bucks a month as salary. I ain't never heard of a fine that high!'

The man leaned closer. 'I said two hundred, mister! Either pay up or he stays in there.'

'Is there a judge in town?'

The sheriff laughed. 'This is a small town.'

Pete said angrily, 'I haven't got that kind of money on me. I'll pay fifty — and I want a receipt for it.'

'I don't sign my name easy, *amigo*.'

'So the dinero goes into your pocket?' Pete said.

Another unpleasant laugh. 'Well, a man has to live, even in a stinkin' hellhole like this.'

'I'll pay fifty and not a cent more,' Pete snapped.

'You've got more than that!' was the sneering answer. 'Empty your pockets and I'll take what you've got.'

Sudden anger against this loud-mouthed representative of the so-called law flared inside Pete Hadfield. Detestation for his breed and irritation over finding the man blocking the way spurred Pete into a rash move. He scooped his Colt from his holster and pointed it at the lawman's head.

'Get the keys and unlock the cell,'

said Pete thickly. 'I'm taking him out — now!'

All the amusement faded from Chet Lancer's big face as he stared at the gun. 'You've made a fool play,' he said slowly. 'You're pointin' that hogleg at a lawman.'

'I know what I'm doin'. Now, just you get on with what I told you.'

'You wouldn't use that gun . . . '

'How the hell do you know?' Pete rapped. 'Are you willing to take the chance I won't shoot?' Now that the move had been made, he had to see it through. 'Get the keys and unlock his cell. I've used this gun before . . . '

'Yeah . . . you handle it like you know how,' the sheriff mumbled. Pete read the growing fear in the sheriff's face. He knew what the lawman was thinking: only a fool would call the play of an unknown man. Baby-faced kids had been known to shoot down lawmen . . .

The sheriff of Santa Arena moved slowly to a drawer in his desk, thinking all the time, wondering how to play this situation. He took out the keys and stared again at Pete. Then with a grim nod, he walked to the door leading to the cell passage. Pete followed him, his Colt jabbing against the man's back. It was a bluff all the way. A gun was used to kill or injure people. Pete had no intention of doing either. But Chet Lancer, so-called sheriff, judged other men by his own ugly standards and that was his weakness. He didn't dare call the bluff.

Lancer walked into the cell passage with Pete right behind him. Two men got slowly to their feet behind iron bars and stared. Harry's eyes met Pete's in surprise. His mouth opened and then clamped shut. The other man, a nondescript drifter, glared at the sheriff and then looked hopefully at Pete Hadfield.

'Get me outa here, feller . . . '

Pete ignored him and Chet Lancer closed in on Harry's cell. The keys jangled on their ring and one was inserted into the lock and turned. The door swung in and Harry slipped through the opening. Pete gave a push and the unprincipled sheriff of Santa Arena was shoved into the cell. The door was locked and the half-brothers strode swiftly out of the passage and through the office. A shout could be heard but it was muffled. In any case, boisterous prisoners were nothing new in a jailhouse.

'Where the hell's my gunbelt?' Harry wanted to know. He spotted it hanging from a rack a moment later. His hat and saddlebags were in another corner. He scooped them up. 'Let's get out of here, brother of mine! Seems like I owe you something.'

'I want a talk with you,' Pete said. 'About Polly Bliss! And I want the truth — all the details!'

'Sure, sure. When we light out of this damn scurvy town. My horse is in the livery.'

There were things to do and they had to be completed in a hurry because there was no sense in lingering any longer in Santa Arena. They brought the horses out of the livery and paid the man. Pete ran along to the hotel, settled for the room he had booked and picked up his rifle, somewhat to the surprise of the desk clerk. Then he rejoined Harry in the dusty street, mounted and rode out of Santa Arena at a fast gallop. They kept up the pace for the best part of a mile then slackened.

'Take it easy,' Harry said. 'This damned animal of mine is blown. I pushed it too far this morning and it ain't had enough rest.'

'Nothing worse than a trail-weary horse,' Pete said. 'Better look after him. We'll have to camp somewhere — it'll be dark soon. But not too close to that damn town.'

'Why the hell did you follow me?' Harry wanted to know.

'You can guess. I want the truth about Polly Bliss.'

'You know it all.'

'She was a girl who had plenty of visitors at night. I've been talkin' to Ted and Martha Smith. You told me twice that you didn't kill her.'

'Forget it,' Harry said.

'Is that an answer? That's all I ever get from you — fool evasive answers!'

'I said forget it! Maybe I should ride off right now and head for the border.'

'Do that and you'll be a hunted man for the rest of your life. Is that the way you want it?'

'I'll be in trouble in any case. You know, Pete, I'm a hardcase. Drink . . . women . . . a wild time and maybe some shootin' — hell, I'll be in big trouble sooner or later anyhow. So it doesn't matter if I'm wanted now. Don't you see? It's like a man who's killed some galoot. He might as well kill again because he can only die for it once.'

Pete blew out his breath in heated exasperation. 'You know and I know that's just a lot of fool talk! You don't have to be a hardcase. And you don't have to run — not if you didn't kill Polly Bliss.'

Harry halted his horse and glared at his brother. 'You're gettin' in my craw, mister. I've got a good mind to take off right now!'

'Tell me how you got that TT horse,' Pete said.

'Go to hell!'

'You know Mick Laverty used to visit Polly Bliss at nights? The way I hear it, all they ever did was argue.'

'Not all the time, brother of mine,' Harry said. 'That little bitch did entertain, you know.'

'Laverty tried to drygulch me. He slaughtered my black near the Comanche War Rocks.'

'You're lucky it was Laverty — he's the worst hand with a gun on either side of the Rio Grande.'

Pete pointed a challenging finger. 'If you didn't kill Polly, who did? I think you know, Harry, but you're holdin' back.'

'They've got me hanged already,' Harry said. 'Two solid citizens of that third-rate town found me with the lady and she was plumb dead. They'll tell you I had my hands around her neck. That was enough for everybody.'

'It's more than enough if you refuse to explain and just offer a lot of fool talk. Listen to me, Harry. I'm convinced that you didn't kill the girl. Was it Mick Laverty?' Harry shrugged.

'If you can pin it on him, I sure won't lose any sleep at night.'

'You're still bein' evasive,' said Pete quietly. 'But I'm gonna learn the truth.'

Suddenly Harry Hadfield pointed at Pete's horse. 'Our brand! You must've seen pa before you rode out after me!'

'Sure. I told him about the attempted lynchin' and the man who hoisted you out of it. And then he told me to let you run wild and free.'

'Changed his tune, huh? Still, he's wiser than you, Pete. And that's the way it's gonna be . . . '

The sun sent fiery rays streaking upwards in its dying show of the day. They rode off the trail because there was no knowing who might come along *en route* to Santa Arena. Minutes after their conversation came to an abrupt end the darkness fell and footing for the animals became precarious on the sand and shale. They rode through a shallow valley where one slope had a spring trickling up through redstone rocks and afforded enough moisture for scrub timber and clumps of grass. Pete looked the place over and met Harry's gaze.

'How about makin' camp here? These nags are tired and we don't want to lame them in a night ride.'

Harry grinned. 'Sure. Why not? Might be the last time we spend a night together. I'll head out at sunup and make for El Paso. Dang me if I won't make that town yet! Guess I'll have to settle for the other side of the Rio Grande when I hit El Paso.'

Pete stared at Harry's bedroll as he took it off the saddle. The striped blanket had come from the TT spread. And he wondered about the gun Harry carried. Who had given it to him?

Pete had food in his saddle-bags.

They made coffee on a small fire, then ate and rolled into their blankets and went to sleep.

Pete Hadfield awakened with the thin rays of the sun on his face and a feeling that something was wrong. Suddenly fear surged through his brain, rousing him instantly. The first thing his eyes registered were two thick legs, clad in brown pants and ending in black leather boots. A man stood over him. And a handgun was aimed down at him.

Sheriff Chet Lancer had outsmarted them. The big Colt looked like a small cannon. The muzzle moved from Pete to Harry.

'Got you two sidewinders! You'll be damn sorry about pullin' a fast one on me! Yes, you'll sure damn well regret it!'

6

The Boy in Town

Two days after Pete Hadfield rode west looking for Harry's trail, Gilbert Hadfield went into Perkinsville. He had to visit the bank, for one thing, so he could get cash for the monthly wages, and he wanted to telegraph a message to the stockyards at Alpine. He knew he'd have to meet Sheriff Tom Sharkey, and that was something he didn't look forward to.

He drove the buckboard into town warily. Right from the start he felt the animosity of the townspeople. Everyone knew that Harry Hadfield was wanted in connection with the murder of Polly Bliss, and everyone knew that Harry had vanished.

The first real show of feeling came as he drove past the Bonanza. A man lounging on the boardwalk stared angrily and shouted, 'Damned Hadfield!'

Then another man cursed him as he entered the bank. 'Where's that skunk son of yours? He's a girl-killer, that's what he is!'

Gilbert Hadfield tightened his lips and pushed his way past the bank's solid oak doors. Inside the building there was the usual deference from the tally clerks. He felt at home in these respectable surroundings where a big oil painting of the bank president hung on a wall and polished oak blocks formed a civilised floor. He got on with his business and left with his valise swollen with money, mostly in small bills, the way the hands liked them.

He walked to the telegraph office and sent his message to Sol Schultz at Alpine, then he walked back along Perkinsville's main stem.

A girl left the draper's store and paused on the boardwalk, glancing at Gilbert Hadfield. He saw her, smiled and halted.

'Why, hello, Cilla! How are you these days? I haven't seen you for some time.'

Cilla Gregg smiled back. She liked the tall, greying man — not merely because he was Pete's father, but because he had an air of authority and seemed a father figure to her.

She missed her own father, dead these past twelve months, a victim of a wasting disease. She and her mother ran a small drapery store through sheer necessity.

'Where's Pete?' she asked. 'Is he in town?'

'No — he — he's out looking for Harry.' The admission brought out all the old grimness in his make-up. He made to pass on but the girl spoke again:

'It's such a dreadful affair, Mr Hadfield. I — I'm so sorry . . . ' Her own dark eyes were filled with concern because she saw him as a lonely man with many troubles. She ran a hand through her dark hair. It fell loosely, black as a raven's wing. Her lustrous hair, along with the colour glowing in her cheeks, and her petite figure and elfin face, made her the prettiest girl in the town. She said, 'I wish I could talk to Pete about this awful thing! I — I — feel so sorry for him . . . '

'Don't concern yourself with it!' he said harshly. 'You're too young — too vital to be even tainted with thoughts about — about — murder! People will have to forget! It's the only way!'

'When will Pete be back? Oh, I do want to see him!'

'I don't know when he'll be back. I didn't want him to ride off. He's stirring up bad blood for himself in this place.'

'But Harry is his brother!'

'Half-brother. A wild hellion, if you'll excuse me, Cilla. He'd be in trouble no matter what. That's his destiny, I guess . . . '

Gilbert Hadfield glanced sharply across the street. A freight wagon passed, cutting off his view momentarily, but he could see the motionless figure of the Indian boy who stared bleakly at him from the opposite boardwalk. It was a fixed stare, completely expressionless. The boy was about fifteen, he thought. He had never seen him before.

Gilbert Hadfield continued his talk with Cilla Gregg. 'I sure hope that you and Pete keep up your friendship . . . '

She coloured in embarrassment. She could have told this man that Pete and she had kissed and exchanged vows of love but perhaps it was too early for that kind of talk. Although maybe it was what he wanted to hear. It was a bit confusing.

Gilbert Hadfield swung his gaze around again and once more he encountered the staring eyes of the Indian boy. The youth was tall for his age and clad in worn buckskin. He was dirty and unkempt, with lank black hair falling down his neck. His expression was so devoid of emotion that it was disconcerting. He was probably one of the town Kiowas. Probably he was staring in simple-minded wonder.

Again Gilbert Hadfield turned to the girl. 'That darned Injun . . . why the devil is he staring like that?'

Cilla laughed, carefree, youthful. 'Oh, that's Curly. Don't you know him? He helps in the livery.'

'I don't want to know him,' Gilbert Hadfield muttered. 'I had enough of Injuns when I was a young man.'

'Oh, Curly is harmless. Poor thing, he's deaf and dumb! Isn't it a pity? He was practically thrown out by his own tribe. They think anyone afflicted is possessed by the devil.'

'In my young days, they were devils themselves . . . '

'But I can communicate with Curly,' the girl went on. 'He seems to like me. We often talk — with our hands — and make signs in the dust. He can't read or write, of course.'

'Maybe the good Lord doesn't intend Indians to read and write although I guess some have managed to do it.' Gilbert Hadfield shrugged. 'I'd better be gettin' along. It's been nice to see you, Cilla.'

He moved away, his face falling into grim lines. Cilla smiled after him, seeing something of Pete Hadfield in him. Just to think of Pete made her glow inside. Perhaps she was just a fool, but Pete was so nice . . .

She half-turned. She had almost forgotten that her mother had asked her to go on a message. As she moved, Curly walked swiftly across the dusty street towards her, dodging a passing horseman. As he approached the girl he waved a hand and she recognized the friendly salute and smiled again.

Curly came close to her. He made mouthing noises and pointed at the departing figure of Gilbert Hadfield. Cilla frowned. She shook her head, her dark hair swishing gracefully.

'What are you trying to tell me, Curly?' She couldn't help talking to the youth although she knew he didn't understand.

He made violent signs with his hands and pointed again down the road at the receding rancher. Then he tugged at her arm. They went around a corner of the frame building and he squatted down and began to draw queer signs in the dust.

The one thing she understood was that all this concerned Gilbert Hadfield, but there was more that she just did not grasp. She fired questions at the Indian youth and sighed at her foolishness. He couldn't hear her. And he couldn't talk, in any language. The Kiowa, with their own traditions, had disowned him, leaving him to his own devices. He lived primitively, earning a little money from odd jobs here and there, mainly in the livery.

'Oh, Curly, what is it?' she sighed. 'What are you trying to tell me? It's about Mr Hadfield, but I don't understand the rest . . . '

Curly was not devoid of intelligence

despite his handicap. He made more crude drawings in the dust and added hand signs. She nodded, concentrating. A detail became clear and then another. The Indian boy pointed at his rough symbols and nodded urgently. He pointed down the main stem at a house. She understood this. Something about the house . . . what was it? He made more hand signs, then his hands went around his throat. What on earth was he doing? It didn't make sense! Really, she just couldn't help him this time! She had helped him with money and food, because she was sorry for any human being so afflicted.

Curly tried again, held her arm, cleared the path of dust. A rangehand passing by stopped, stared and shook his head at the odd sight. Curly made more patterns in the earth and pointed. Then, suddenly, one salient fact stood out as clear as if she were reading a book. Cilla Gregg almost recoiled in horror. As Curly made more crude drawings, the gist of his effort at communication flashed dramatically through her mind. She knew at last, all too terribly, what the Indian boy was trying to tell her.

She was probably the only one in Perkinsville who would be able to understand Curly — or believe him!

* * *

As Gilbert Hadfield had feared, he bumped into the sheriff. Tom Sharkey had been drinking in Sal's Place and had just walked back into the warm afternoon. He was a round, jovial man who liked Sal's good beer, maintaining that yeast was the source of vitality. Maybe that was true, for Tom Sharkey had plenty of drive despite his bulk. He smiled at the rancher. 'Why, hello, Gilbert.'

The rancher tensed, his shoulder muscles tightening as he squared up. 'What are you doin' about Harry?' he asked bluntly.

The sheriff sighed. 'A Wanted poster goes out today.'

'He's a young fool. And as for that girl — '

'She was playin' fast and loose, I know.'

'Are you makin' inquiries, Tom?'

'Sure. I've been all over the durned town. That girl sure knew some men — a lot more than some folks thought.'

'Have you talked to that hellion, Mick Laverty? He tried to stir up a lynch mob. And he tried to kill Pete — shot his horse to hell from under him.'

'Is Pete makin' a charge?'

'Maybe not,' Gilbert Hadfield muttered. 'He's out looking for Harry, although I told him to forget it.'

'Where's he gone? Does he know where to find Harry?'

'He doesn't, and neither do I, so you can quit askin' me to do your job for you, Sheriff. You ought to have a new deputy.'

'Yeah. The town committee are considerin' some galoots. Might be better if they paid more for the job. I don't want another skunk like Laverty! He's got no real respect for law and order.'

'He knew that girl, too.'

Sheriff Tom Sharkey glanced at Hadfield. 'Are you suggestin' that he killed her?'

'Could be.'

'Harry was found with the girl and she was dead. Harry ran off. He gets brought back — Pete helpin' — and then some smart cuss hauls him out of the hands of a lynch mob and he ain't been seen since!'

'You wouldn't want a lynchin' in this town, would you?'

'No, I sure wouldn't! And you?' Tom Sharkey gave Hadfield a piercing look. 'He's your son. You'd want justice for him, too, not a necktie party.'

'Any decent man wants justice.'

'Sure, sure. And that's what I aim to see done. When we get Harry — alive, I hope — he'll get his fair hearin'. Judge Harlan has promised me a full trial with a local jury.'

'They'd be ready to hang him before they start,' said Gilbert Hadfield harshly. 'He's better runnin' free and wild.'

'I'd better warn you, Gilbert,' said the sheriff, all his joviality gone, 'that aidin' and abettin' Harry to escape is against the law and I'd come down hard on it!'

'I know that! I sent Pete out to get him! Now I'm not so sure that it was a wise move. Harry is maybe better off ridin' wild and free. He's a wild boy and he'd be in trouble anywhere. A man can't escape his destiny, you know that, Tom.'

The sheriff smiled and slapped the other man's shoulder. 'Now, don't let it get you down. The best thing for Harry is to get a fair hearin', so it's all out in the open.'

'I don't know,' Gilbert Hadfield mumbled. 'He won't be caged, I tell you that. He's a man who yearns for far horizons — free and wild!' He turned away, muttering. 'Yes, sir, free and wild. That's the best way for Harry . . . '

He returned to the spot where he had hitched the buckboard horse. He climbed to the seat and took up the whip. Hadfield was about to gather up the reins when a man sprang from out of a nearby alley and pulled the horse's head down. His surly mouth was twisted in hate. His mean eyes blazed. His small, insignificant body was crouched in anger.

'You low-down skunk! You yeller-bellied father of a girl-killin' skunk. How do you get the nerve to show your face in town!' Wally Bliss was almost spitting. He had been drinking; his face bore an alcoholic flush.

'Get out of my way!' Anger tore into Gilbert Hadfield. Rage was never far away in his makeup, and age hadn't mellowed it to any degree. 'You damned scum — get! Let go of that horse!'

He knew the small man as the brother of the dead girl; a drifter who worked only when funds ran low. That was his total knowledge of the man.

'I reckon you're hiding that dirty son of yours!' shrilled Wally Bliss. 'You — big man, Hadfield — why, you're as stinkin' rotten as your polecat son! I know you ranchers . . . you get rich and you try to lord it over the likes of me! You turned me down once for a job, old man!'

'I don't even remember you!' Gilbert Hadfield snarled. He glanced to the right and left. Some men and two women had stopped on the boardwalk to stare at the scene. He intensely disliked this kind of humiliation. He turned and shouted angrily at the small young man. 'Get your hand off that horse! By hell, if you don't I'll whip you free!'

Wally Bliss, full of cheap booze, produced a Bowie knife. 'I'll slice this goddamn harness and make you walk, big man! You fathered a damned girl-killer, Hadfield!'

Wally Bliss made a sudden move with the knife as if to hack at the leathers on the shafts. But Gilbert Hadfield flicked the horsewhip at the man. The long thong snicked wickedly around Bliss' neck, almost choking him. The rancher jerked the whip back and Wally Bliss staggered back, the knife falling from his hand. He made a dive for his knife and the whip slashed at him again. The stinging pain burned through him and he tried to clutch at the thong. The whip drew back again and Gilbert Hadfield lost control and proceeded to horsewhip Bliss unmercifully, hissing with rage at the humiliating situation the drifter had gotten him into. Red welts appeared on Bliss' face and neck. As Wally Bliss put up his hands to shield his face, the whip lashed them viciously.

Then Sheriff Tom Sharkey came running, gun in hand, his voice angry.

'You two — cut it out! Hadfield, stop that right now! You hear me? Stop it, I say!'

Gasping for breath, Gilbert Hadfield felt the rage drain from him. He stood on the buckboard footrest, the whip hanging limply. He still felt hatred of this small, dirt-scuffed drifter, but the killing anger flooded away, back into the dark recesses of his body, controlled at last. He hated Wally Bliss for the things he had said and for staging this bitter scene.

'What the hell got into you, Gilbert?' the sheriff roared.

'This scum . . . insulted me . . . threatened to cut my harness . . . ' The rancher turned, appealed to the crowd. 'Didn't you hear him? Didn't you see him with the knife?' People just melted away, heads down. One man spat. 'Hadfield, huh! The name stinks!'

A woman, her face white with fear, screamed, 'It was his son who killed that poor girl!'

Wally Bliss snarled, 'This mangey skunk attacked me, Sheriff! Just because I said he's hidin' his boy!'

'Is he? Can you prove that?' Tom Sharkey looked angrily at the pint-sized man. 'If you can't prove it, why don't you keep your trap shut! It takes two to stir up trouble! I could run you both in for disturbin' the peace.'

'I'm goin' back home, Sheriff,' said Gilbert Hadfield grimly. 'I've had enough of this damned town! If you want to make charges, go ahead.'

'I'm warnin' you both — '

Wally Bliss was still hazed with drink and had no control over himself. 'He ain't gettin' away with it! By hell, looks like there's one law for the poor and one for the rich! His dirty, stinkin' son kills my sister and he whips me! I aim to get even — see if I don't!'

'Right now you can get off the street,' warned the sheriff. 'You've been at the hooch.'

'Yeah, well you ain't no teetotaller and I don't need you to tell me what to do. There ain't no real law in this town for a poor man — or a poor girl — so I know just what to do. I've got pards . . . yes, sir. Me and Mick Laverty will fix the Hadfields good and proper, you'll see . . . '

'Get back to that shack of yours and

sleep it off,' advised the sheriff. 'You sound like a loco Apache. You don't know what you're sayin'. Now get!'

But Wally Bliss nurtured all his murderous thoughts as he staggered along the street.

7

Bury the Man!

'You can drop them gunbelts for a start,' Sheriff Chet Lancer said. 'You boys don't take no chances, huh? You sleep with your hardware all nice and handy. Well, drop 'em or I'll drop you!'

Pete Hadfield was on his feet along with his brother. They had crawled out of the blankets at the threat of the big sheriff's gun and now they were itching to go for their Colts. But each knew it was the sure way to a quick death. One thing was sure; Chet Lancer palmed his artillery with the deft touch of a gunman. He would shoot without compunction and rely on his badge to justify his actions.

Pete began to unbuckle his gunbelt. The morning sun was strong already and the spring made bubbling sounds behind them. Harry grinned and eased off his gunbelt with tantalising slowness, keeping his mocking eyes on the big sheriff from Santa Arena.

'Lawman, you sure hit the trail bright and early!' He laughed.

'I got started before first light. Picked up your fresh hoofmarks with a lighted torch and knew you were on this trail.'

'You know, you should get a bonus,' Harry Hadfield jeered. His gunbelt dropped with a thud. Pete's gunbelt had already slid to the ground.

'You two step clear of that hardware,' Chet Lancer ordered. 'We'll do this nice and orderly, takin' our time. I figure you boys ain't what you say you are. Ed Brown and cousin? Bulldust!'

Pete drew in a deep breath. 'Now look here, Sheriff, all this is only because I wouldn't pay the two hundred dollars. You know that was too much for a fracas between two gents.'

'Gunfightin' in town is against the law,' said Chet Lancer. 'A man got shot up and the peace was disturbed. But it ain't just that.'

'I'll pay you the fifty I first offered,' said Pete quickly.

Lancer shook his head. 'I got hunches about you two. You're too damned anxious to get this galoot out of jail. So what's it all about? You ain't on any Wanted list that I've got — but that don't mean you ain't on one somewhere. Somethin' tells me I'm on to something good for Chet Lancer. Now what can that be, boys? What have you done? You're headin' for the border, ain't you? And that TT brand — now damn me if I won't start makin' inquiries about that brand!'

Pete frowned at this arrogant representative of law and order. He cursed their choice of camp. The place had been too easy to find. Obviously someone had released the sheriff from the cell and he was the headstrong type who didn't give up.

'All right, next move,' Chet Lancer said. He walked carefully to his patient horse. It was a big-boned animal that suited his heavy frame. He unhooked a short length of rope and tossed it to Pete Hadfield. 'I'm all prepared, gents. Now tie his wrists behind his back, *amigo*. That rope is just the right length.' He grinned at Pete. 'You — get on with it! I want your pal tied up first. He looks a bit mean to me.'

Under the threat of the big Colt, there seemed no way out. Pete approached Harry. His brother obligingly placed his hands behind his back. As Pete fumbled with the rope, Harry whispered, 'We've got to get him!'

'How?'

'Fool around . . . work slow . . . talk to him . . . get him to come close up . . .'

Sheriff Chet Lancer's eyes narrowed to slits of cold steel. 'Cut out that damned whisperin'!'

Harry stared back at him, laughing. 'I'm just callin' you a few choice names, *amigo*! You don't mind me talkin' to my brother, do you?'

'Brother, eh?' The sheriff sneered. 'Not cousins now — brothers! It figures. There's somethin' about the cut of your jaws.'

'Hell, that slipped out,' muttered Harry, almost to himself.

Chet Lancer made a threatening move with his gun. 'Have you got his damned hands tied yet?'

'Tryin',' said Pete, and he made fumbling motions with the rope against Harry's back. Harry kept his wrists together, his hands bunched into knotted fists which showed his temper was only just under control. Harry inched forward, making it look as if he was teetering on his feet.

'You two jaspers are goin' back to Santa Arena,' stated the sheriff. 'I got me two empty cells. While you're in 'em, I aim to make inquiries about that brand on them nags. You're charged with breakin' jail and stickin' a gun on a lawman.'

'Lawman!' Harry jeered. 'How much will it take to buy you off?'

'You ain't got any dinero . . . '

'No — you took it from me when you marched me into your little jail, and I ain't forgot that.'

'How much did you have, Harry?' Pete stopped fumbling with the rope and looked up.

Harry moved another few inches forward, as if Pete was pushing him. 'I had a hundred dollars.'

'Where the devil did you get that much money?'

'I had it hidden away . . . '

'But where? You were spirited away from the lynch mob without a penny on you. And I think you know the identity of the rider who took you. You must know — you can't ride behind a man and not know him.'

Harry frowned darkly. 'You're asking as many questions as that pesky sheriff.'

'We're gonna have it out in the open,' Pete grated.

Chet Lancer suddenly bawled. 'You two are tryin' some fool play! Ain't you got them wrists tied yet?' He stepped to the side, his big boots digging at the sandy earth. He went into a wary crouch and with two strides he circled the two prisoners. As he moved, Harry inched around so that his hands were still hidden from the sheriff's view. Pete had to turn with him.

Sheriff Chet Lancer halted. 'All right! So it's trick stuff! You got one minute, *amigo*, to really tie them wrists. If you don't, I'll shoot this brother of yours to high hell!'

Pete Hadfield was sure the attempt to play around was doomed, but Harry whispered, 'Inch forward while I hand him some more fool talk.'

Pete gave a convincing impression of tying Harry's hands behind his back, jerking him bodily, so that their feet stole another six inches of space between them and the lawman.

The sheriff was watching with tight-lipped anger. His suspicion that all was not going to plan made him creep forward, an involuntary act which he did not realize was bringing him nearer to the two younger men. His boots made scuffing sounds in the earth; his gun stayed level.

'All right, I'm coming to have a close look at that rope!'

As his body swayed, Harry said softly, 'Ram me at him! Now!'

There was no time for Pete to protest that this was courting sudden death. With an inward groan, he rammed Harry forward with terrific force, his hands against the small of his back. At the same time, Harry dived for the sheriff's feet.

It was a terrible gamble because they had to beat the gun. The big lawman triggered just as Harry's outstretched hands reached his legs. The bullet cut through Harry's dark hair, only missing his skull because of the angle of his dive. A second shot spat after the first — but at that moment Harry's hands had wrapped around the thick legs of the lawman and had begun to knock him off balance. The second slug dug into the earth, again only inches from its target.

As Pete had rammed his brother forward he had also dived, knowing that the sheriff's gun would send out hot lead. As Harry sent the sheriff staggering back, Pete scrambled forward on all fours. Then he launched himself at the lawman as the man dug his heels into the earth in an attempt to keep his balance. Pete's hands grabbed a leg. He tugged. Chet Lancer twisted around as he tried desperately to remain upright. He swung his gun again, pointing it down at the two men at his feet.

But Harry was just a split-second ahead of the move, knowing full well that the gun had to be disposed of in some way. As the lawman angled the gun down, Harry Hadfield thrust his hands up and grabbed at the big weapon. The Colt spat flame and lead and the slug hissed past Harry's face. He felt the heat and smelled the gunsmoke, then he wrapped his hands around the warm metal of the gun and twisted the weapon from the other man's grip.

Chet Lancer fell hard. His face rammed into the dust and he roared his rage. The two Hadfields jumped on him and stopped his attempt to roll clear. He writhed and bucked viciously but Pete and Harry kept him down, grinding his face into the dust. His hat was flung in one direction and his gun was some five yards away. Then, with Pete safely holding the man, his arms twisted up behind his back, Harry strode over to his gunbelt, plucked the Colt from leather and rammed the weapon into the big lawman's side.

'Quit strugglin', mister! We've got you dead to rights!' The man subsided, hugging the ground and dragging harshly for breath as anger distorted his features. His fury agonized him. But he was helpless.

'Reckon this length of rope will come in mighty useful,' said Pete. 'Now I think we'll tie your wrists.'

'You two hellions will pay for this!'

'Shut your damned lip!' Harry spat out. 'You were all set to fill us with lead!'

'I'm the law. You'll be sorry about this, I swear it!'

'Plenty of things I might live to regret,' said Harry. 'You're only one of 'em.'

Within minutes the sheriff was trussed and sitting up, glaring around him but unable to retaliate.

'Are we gonna set him on his horse and point him in the direction of Santa Arena?' Pete asked.

'He'll talk . . .'

'Ain't much we can do about that. And you? How about comin' back to town and clearin' up this whole mess?'

'Leave it alone. I won't be comin' back, Pete. Leave everything the way it is. That's the best way, brother of mine.'

Pete Hadfield gripped Harry's arm. 'With every word you say I know there's somethin' wrong. Who killed Polly Bliss?'

'I did. She was a rotten little bitch.'

'I've heard you say you didn't kill her.'

'Just fool talk, *amigo*! You know me — I'm always tryin' to make a monkey outa somebody!'

'No,' Pete said. 'Some galoot spirited you away from that lynch mob and that someone had good reasons. Now give me some talk about that man!'

Harry swung around. 'Get out of my hair!'

'I want you back in town — talkin' sense in a courtroom.'

Harry Hadfield gave the glowering lawman a swift glance. 'Shut up,' he said to Pete. 'You'll say too much in a minute. Do you want that skunk to know everything?'

Pete compressed his lips, then he buckled on his gunbelt and washed his face in the spring. He felt a bit better but hungry. They needed grub before they moved on, but would he return to the TT ranch alone? Had his long trip been for nothing?

Chet Lancer suddenly spoke up. 'By

thunder, I'll remember you two coyotes for a long time! I'll make it my business to hound you down, see if I don't. I got that brand to work on. I'll ride around, do some talkin' and find out where you two came from. Brothers, huh? You won't be hard to locate and when I do, I'll get you. I'm an accredited lawman and folks will listen.'

Harry Hadfield went over to the man. He eased his gun from his holster and allowed it to drop back suggestively. 'Maybe it'd be a good idea if you weren't around to do any talkin', feller!'

Pete stared hard. 'Harry — ' The name slipped out before he could stop it. He swallowed and glanced at the sheriff. The man wasn't slow on the uptake.

'Harry, huh?' he sneered. 'What's the rest? Thanks for the tip, *hombre*. I'll get you. You busted a man outa my jail and roughed me up. I'll get you . . . '

Harry Hadfield laughed. 'Maybe we should let you walk back to Santa

Arena. Who knows? You might never make it.'

'Put him on his horse now and get rid of him,' Pete said.

'Not until after we've had some grub. I'm kind of peckish. Maybe it's a good idea to let him walk. He might do some hard thinkin' and change his mind about comin' after us at some future date not that I'll be around to welcome the ugly bastard.'

'It would've been a lot better if you'd stayed out of trouble in Santa Arena,' Pete said.

'Sure, but there were two rannies who were tryin' to be funny at my expense and I wasn't in a humorous mood.'

'You have a gift for gettin' into trouble.' Pete looked around for some bits of wood. There were broken branches further up the slope in the scrub. 'Let's get a fire started. My guts are rumblin'.'

While the two brothers gathered wood and dried roots, the sheriff of

Santa Arena glared. He stared at the horses — two big animals with the TT brand marks — and had an idea. It might lead nowhere, but maybe he could make things hard for the two men who had bested him. True, his hands were tied, but his feet were free. Presumably the two intended to put him on his saddle and let him go. It was reassuring to know they weren't outright killers, but that point merely encouraged him to start a new play. He looked at them again, narrow-eyed and evil, and saw that the two were halfway up the scrub-filled slope.

Chet Lancer got to his feet, looked again at the two TT horses and noted they were loosely tied to a stunted scrub tree which was no more than four feet in height and blackened as if scarred by lightning. He walked over to the horses, turned his bound hands to the loosely looped leathers, and after some moments of fumbling succeeded in freeing the reins of the two animals. With another glance at the backs of the two distant men, he walked to his own horse. The animal stood meekly, having long ago been dominated by him.

Getting into the saddle wasn't easy with his hands bound, but Chet Lancer had spent a lifetime on horseback and any trick with a horse came readily to him. With one neatly balanced swing upwards with his right leg, his left foot firmly in a stirrup, he hit the saddle and with his big thighs gripped the ribcage of the horse. The animal jigged a bit, then he rowelled the horse straight at the two animals bearing the TT brand.

Pete and Harry whipped around and stared as they heard the rapid tattoo of hoofs. The two TT horses, spooked into sudden fear, were rearing. The next second the animals wheeled on springy haunches and leaped off in the same direction as Chet Lancer and his big horse. As their hoofs drummed at the earth, Harry whipped out his sixgun and fired.

Harry's first two shots missed by a hair's breadth, then he ran down the slope, sending off shots as the horses and the solitary rider charged down the valley.

'Get him!' Harry shouted. 'He's leavin' us stranded!'

The gap was widening between them and the animals. The hardcase sheriff was low on his horse, legs tight against the animal's ribs.

Harry threw the last slug at the escaping man. He kept running, trying to reload at the same time. If the lawman got out of range, he had licked them! Harry shouted to Pete, 'Shoot, damn you! Do you want to walk?'

Pete raised his gun and raced along the shale and sand valley, dodging cactus growth and scrub bush. He levelled his gun, hesitated, and then fired two shots. At the same moment Harry finished reloading, whipped up the gun and triggered swiftly. Any results would be pure luck at this range, with a swiftly running man firing at a galloping horse.

Harry's volley of shots mingled with

the blast from Pete's Colt. Chet Lancer kept hugging the back of his frightened horse — and then, slowly, the man toppled from the saddle. His left boot stayed in the stirrup and he was dragged along. Then the foot came clear and the man lay prone on the flat earth, face down, motionless.

Pete and Harry raced up to the sheriff and stared down at him for a moment. Harry rolled the man over. Immediately they saw the hole in the side of the man's head, and Harry let him drop back.

'Holster that hogleg, brother of mine,' he muttered. 'He's dead — buzzard bait.' Harry caught Pete's gaze and he jeered, 'Was it your bullet or mine?'

Pete Hadfield nearly dropped his gun as fear clawed at his stomach and he stared at the body. He had carried a gun for some years, but only as protection in a savage land that demanded a man carried the means to deal out death. He had never killed a man. Now, looking down, he hated what he saw. Somebody's life had been snuffed out, as if he meant nothing in this world. And whose bullet had reached the sheriff? Who had killed him?

'Don't look so scared. He'd have run off our horses and left us to walk in this damned wasteland, to likely die of thirst.'

'You fired at the same time I did.'

'Sure. We got the sidewinder, and just as well. He'd have gone back to town and then come hellin' after us with a posse. He knew our horse brands, too, and that was no good.'

'He was a lawman,' Pete said. 'We're in real bad . . . '

'I'm in bad in any case,' Harry said. 'All right, don't look so plumb disturbed, Pete. I'll take the blame for this if anyone ever gets around to throwin' blame.'

'It could've been one of my shots,' muttered Pete. His young face showed his horror. 'I could've killed him. Good God, Harry . . . see what it's all led to! He's dead — and he was a sheriff!'

'A louse, too. Now snap out of it and help me round up those horses. They'll be all the way to El Paso if we don't stop 'em.'

But in fact the TT mounts had slowed and they stood uncertainly a few hundred yards along the valley. As Pete and Harry approached, the horses cocked expectant ears, recognizing their masters. The two men grabbed at the reins, mounted and went off after the third horse. Harry wanted time to consider what to do with the animal.

With the third horse on a lead rope, they rode back to the camp where the bedrolls still lay.

'I'm hungry,' said Harry. 'Damn that man! Well, we'll bury him and light out. I'll head off to El Paso and you can hit the dust for home. End of the line, Pete.'

Pete Hadfield nodded helplessly. He was watching Harry, seeing the recklessness grow in him. There was contempt for the law and no consideration for other people. This waywardness would grow as he stayed on Wanted lists. Harry would become a hardened no-good, running all his life. And all because of a girl. And now a dead sheriff! That was the hellish part — the dead lawman — because it involved the two of them.

They had to work hard and fast, burying the dead man. It wasn't for them, Pete thought grimly, to take the open course of bringing the dead man back to town and making explanations. That was entirely ruled out and he hated it.

They ate a hurried meal of jerky and bread washed down with water. They couldn't spare the time to light the fire.

'All right,' Harry said. 'Let's go. We part right here, Pete.'

Pete nodded, walked close to his brother — and then whipped the gun from his holster. 'No — you're goin' back with me, Harry. Back to Perkinsville and a fair hearin'. The runnin' has stopped!'

8

The Only Way

Harry Hadfield laughed in his brother's face. 'What in tarnation do you figure you're doin'? You can't make me go back with you. Hell, you'll have to shoot me first!' And Harry laughed again.

'I came after you in order to get explanations,' said Pete harshly. 'I haven't had any that satisfy me. Now there's only one way; you'll talk sense in Perkinsville . . . '

'You don't know what you're doin',' Harry said slowly. 'I'm not goin' back.' He looked down at the handgun pointed at his body. 'I'll tell you one thing, Pete, goin' back is a lot worse than runnin'. Now put that hogleg away — hand it back and we'll part. You ain't shootin' me.'

Pete Hadfield stepped back a few paces and Harry searched his face, his grin fading. 'Damned if you ain't serious! Pete, it's no good. I'll hang — make no mistake about that!'

'Did you kill Polly Bliss?'

'I killed her.'

Pete's eyes bored into his brother's, right past the façade of his reckless expression and deep down into his soul. 'You're lyin',' he said. 'Come on, we'll start back. Get on your horse.'

'You can't carry it through,' said Harry grimly. 'You can't shoot me — you can't tie me up — and if you figure to knock me unconscious with a gunbutt let me tell you I'll dance out of reach until we both get mighty tired.'

'Pa told me to let you go wild and free,' said Pete, 'but I don't see the sense to that. It's a dead certainty that the law will catch up with you some day and by then you'll have made every-thing worse. Right now we're in a heap of trouble. We've killed a man . . . '

'I killed him,' said Harry carelessly. 'If

you've got a conscience, brother of mine, just let it be said that I killed the rannigan.'

'You're going back with me, Harry.' Pete's voice wavered a bit. He held the gun cocked and ready to fire. 'I mean it. We'll get to the bottom of all this. There's things you haven't told me — I know it . . . '

'You're a damn fool. You just never grew up, Pete!'

'There are only two years between us,' Pete said.

'Yeah? And ten years of hellin' around on my side! Women? Hell, you've known only Cilla Gregg! Drink? You hardly ever touch the stuff! Gamble? D'you know what it's like to lay down everything you own?'

'I'm layin' a helluva lot right now on my feelin' that you're tryin' to fool me, Pa, the law and all the others.'

'I've told you — it ain't gonna work.' Harry shuffled to the side. 'Drop that hardware or give it back — I want out

150

of here! I'm sick of the whole thing, brother!'

'Get on your horse and promise you won't try to escape.'

Harry laughed. 'Hell, forget it. When I hit that horse I'm ridin' out like a bit of greasewood in a high wind.'

'You're goin' back to Perkinsville and a hearin' where you'll have to tell the truth.'

'I don't have to be doin' anything. All right, so you've made your play, Pete, and it didn't work. Let me get that bedroll on my horse and ride out.'

Pete watched his brother fix the bedroll behind the saddle on his mount, then Harry vaulted into leather. 'I'm off, *amigo*! Care to give me back my gun? I might need it.'

Pete Hadfield felt the awful approach of the moment of truth, a sickening sense of fatalism. He had to face up to harsh reality and back his convictions with action. Talk was cheap — and Harry was doing his best to prove it. Every word he uttered, his whole attitude, indicated that he didn't believe Pete would stand up to grim hometruths. Harry was sure it was all words . . . just words . . .

'You're not ridin' off,' Pete Hadfield clipped out. 'I figure there's only one way to stop you.'

Harry's eyes gleamed uncertainly, just for a moment, then his jaunty confidence asserted itself. 'There is, Pete, but you won't do it.'

The gun spat lead and reddish flame. The smell of gunsmoke permeated the air and while it eddied up to Pete's nostrils Harry yelped in pain and clasped at his thigh. His horse jigged in fear, turning right around, its eyes rolling. Pete ran forward, grabbed the reins and held the animal's head down.

'All right, Harry, you ain't goin' anywhere alone. Not with a leg wound. You'd lose blood, fall off your horse and maybe die if you didn't come across help. And folks get mighty leery about men with gunshot wounds . . . '

Harry groaned. 'You fool! You damn

fool! What the hell have you done?'

'Shot you. I had to.'

'By God, look at the blood . . . '

'Sure. You'll need a doc to get that slug out and there ain't one in Kinton or Ramsy so you'll have to go clear to Perkinsville.'

'You could take the slug out.'

'We haven't time,' Pete gritted. 'Now I don't need your word — we're just ridin' out, together.'

'It's two days' hard goin' to get home.' Harry groaned again and ran a hand over his thigh. Blood had seeped thickly into the cloth of his pants and his hand came away red and sticky. He flung Pete a scowl. 'By God, you did it! Pete, you fool, now everything is fouled up. You and your damned high-mindedness!'

Pete whipped off his bandanna. He wrapped it around his brother's wounded thigh, tightly, and stepped back. He got his bedroll stowed away and then he mounted his horse. In silence the two men rode away.

For some miles there was a grim silence between the brothers as the horses jogged along. Harry's lips were clenched against the pain of his wound. Pete had been right; Harry was not contemplating riding off into the unknown in this state. He was a virtual prisoner.

But Harry's mind was full of wild conjecture. He knew they would pass through Kinton and Ramsy, unless Pete figured to avoid the towns. But would he? They needed food. At the end of the first day they had skirted Ramsy, the first sign of human habitation on the ride back. Pete had decided not to enter the place because of the lawless hellions he had seen the first time through. They camped some miles out in a gully that offered some comfort in the way of shelter and water. Pete lit a fire of brushwood. He opened his only can of beans and placed thick slices of bacon on his small, blackened frying-pan. They had coffee in tin mugs and some more dry bread. They were both hungry and Harry was feeling weak through loss of blood. The wound had caked with congealed blood and trail dust and looked bad. Pete examined it and wondered if he should try to take out the slug. There was the risk of infection with the bullet still lodged in the flesh, but his skill at this kind of doctoring was strictly limited. It wasn't every day that an ordinary rangehand was faced with the task of performing surgery, even of the crudest nature. It was a job for a medico — and as he'd told Harry, there wasn't one in this vast stretch of semi-arid land until they reached Perkinsville. Pete looked at Harry.

'Are you feelin' all right?'

'Just fine and dandy,' Harry said with deep sarcasm. He lay back against his saddle, his leg outstretched. 'I like it this way, you damn fool!'

'Think you can make it to town?'

'Yeah. You can sling me over the saddle if I get to the stage where I can't sit on it.'

'I don't like your blasted fool talk!

Do you ever talk sense?'

'You oughta know . . . I'm your brother!' Harry's gleaming eyes suddenly soured. 'We've got to reach Perkinsville now, that's for sure, after your fool trick.'

On the second day they stopped at Kinton and Pete bought some beans, bacon and flour at the ramshackle store as Harry sat sullenly in the saddle outside the place, with the heat rising from the dull yellow ground in waves. Pete came out of the store, strapped on the saddle-bags and hit the saddle, urging the tired horse forward. In this way, with a curious glance from the storekeeper, they headed for Perkinsville, knowing they wouldn't reach it before nightfall because the horses couldn't be pushed in this heat.

They spent another night at a secluded spot, near a chaparral clump, with a hill rising behind them. They had full stomachs that night, watching the full moon ride high in the sky and listening to a distant coyote howling.

'We hit town tomorrow,' Pete muttered. 'We ain't calling at the ranch. You need a doc first.'

'I need a drink — and I don't mean water! I need a woman, too — one like Polly! Say, she was some girl. Ain't easy to find 'em built like that . . . kinda puts a man off ordinary women — you know, the straight kind who want only wedding bells . . . like Cilla . . . '

'You can quit talkin' about Cilla like that.'

'She is something special . . . ' There was a hint of grudging admiration in Harry's voice. 'Do you aim to marry her, Pete, after I get the hangnoose treatment?'

'You're tryin' to ride me.'

'I guess so. Some mean streak inside me. Say, we two ain't much alike, are we? Brother? Huh! Only in name.'

'Get some sleep. You need it and there's nothing else to do.'

They lay still, each with his own thoughts, and eventually Harry fell into a troubled sleep. Pete did not drowse off because sombre thoughts raced in his brain, tormenting him, challenging him. As Harry had rightly said, he was young and had never helled around the saloons. The death of Chet Lancer troubled him; the rights and wrongs of Polly Bliss' death was another sore point. Had the girl deserved to die? No, of course not! Was he right to drag Harry back like this? If they hanged Harry, would it haunt him for the rest of his life?

His thoughts were broken as Harry began to mutter in his sleep. At first Pete took little notice beyond realizing grimly that the wound was troubling his brother. Then he heard clearly, 'Polly . . . dear little Polly . . . double-dealin' bitch . . . you damn Jezebel . . . you . . . you . . . '

There was a pause. Pete felt his flesh freeze as more chaotic muttering came. ' . . . I wouldn't kill you . . . no . . . no . . . but he did . . . strangled . . . strangled . . . strangled . . . oh — God — God — God!'

Pete Hadfield shivered. Now he knew that Harry had not killed the wretched girl, that there was some terrible mystery behind it all. For a moment he dreaded hearing any more of Harry's wild ramblings but they came just the same and he had to listen.

' . . . ain't no good . . . can't let it happen . . . yeah yeah . . . I — I — killed her — yeah . . . that's it! Got to be . . . got to be . . . '

Pete rolled over and grabbed his brother's arm and shook him. 'Turn it off, Harry! For God's sake, you don't know what you're sayin'. I don't want to hear any more.'

Harry opened his eyes. 'What's the matter? Somebody comin'?'

Pete drew in a deep breath. 'No. I — I thought I heard a noise. Forget it. Go to sleep . . . '

Day dawned just like it had the other mornings, with the sun peering above the horizon, thin and without the heat that would come later. Pete got stiffly to his feet, looked around and felt cold.

Sombre-faced as he recalled last night's rambling words from Harry, he swiftly built a fire, heated water and made coffee. He needed the hot liquid to chase away an inward chill that wasn't entirely due to the coldness of the morning.

Harry was aroused and he pulled himself clear of his bedroll. He looked bad. His beard was black around his chin and his eyes were sunken. He knew they had to get medical attention soon. The devil had been fever-burned out of him. With only a few muttered words, he drank coffee and then ate bacon and flapjacks. Later Pete had to help him to his horse.

They rode into Perkinsville just after midday, two dusty, weary men on head-drooping horses. Before they reached the sheriff's office, shouts came from some onlookers. 'There's Harry Hadfield!' And, 'Two Hadfields, by thunder!'

'He needs a doc,' Pete snapped. 'He's got a flesh wound in the leg. Help me in

160

with him, will you?'

The sheriff obliged and Harry was taken to a cell and placed on the bunk. An oldster who did odd jobs around the law office was sent in haste to fetch Doc Kelly. Harry lay back and tried to kindle his old, mocking smile, but he could manage only a sick grimace.

Doc Kelly was found, after some delay, because he was attending to a childbirth, and that, to him, came before fools who got themselves shot. He bustled into the jail, a wizened little man with a carpetbag. 'Don't take no skill to dig out lead! Now a baby can be very tricky! This the galoot?'

Doc Kelly worked efficiently. He got the bullet out, then made a curt remark about possible infection. 'But he'll be all right. Flesh heals — now ain't that a miracle? We'd all be dead from poison if it didn't! I'll come back tomorrow to look at this. Right now I'm busy.'

Sheriff Tom Sharkey quietly ushered Pete out of the cell and locked the door. 'All right, maybe you can tell me where you found him, and what he said about that dead girl.'

'I'll make a statement before the trial,' said Pete, 'but not right now. I've got things to do — my father to see — a lawyer to find and some other details — '

'All right,' returned the sheriff. 'But the feeling in this town is that the trial will be held inside of two days. It was a girl that got killed, Pete — a pretty, young girl and she didn't die nicely. She was strangled. People don't like that . . . '

Pete Hadfield went into the street. He was collecting the reins of his horse from the tie-rail when he became aware that Cilla Gregg was standing beside him. 'Oh, hello, Cilla . . . '

'I heard you'd just got into town. Someone came into the store . . . ' She looked down at her feet, unhappy, confusion stamped on her pretty young face.

'I had to bring him in, Cilla.' His lips formed stiff words. His face was dirty and cracked from trail dust and sun. 'I don't think Harry killed that girl. She was no good and knew a lot of men. Sure, he let everybody think he'd killed her, but he didn't.'

She nodded. 'Pete, I'm so sorry for you . . . '

He touched her arm. 'Don't worry about it, Cilla. I'll work like mad to prove Harry's innocence — although for some mad reason he doesn't want it that way.'

She looked pityingly into his face, words impossible to find. She didn't know what to say to him, how to even begin to convey her information.

'He didn't kill her,' he said again. 'He's a fool, taking the blame as he is. I know he didn't kill her . . . '

'You're right,' Cilla Gregg choked. 'He didn't!'

9

'He Was Always a Wild Buckaroo . . . '

Pete Hadfield stared at the girl. His dusty, sweat-caked face was a grim mask. He was weary and his brain was swirling with confusion. 'What do you mean, Cilla?'

'He didn't kill that girl . . . ' Her pretty face was drawn. 'He — he didn't!'

'Do you know something?' Pete asked.

'I — I can't tell you.' Fear assailed her. The words she had rehearsed ever since she had 'talked' to Curly, the Indian boy, in his sign language, seemed to leave her mind and her heart was filled with dread. She began to stammer.

'You can't tell me?' Pete echoed. He frowned in bewilderment. 'Now look,

Cilla, I'm damn tired and I'm sick at heart and I just don't get it. For the Lord's sake, talk sense! You don't know anything about that girl and Harry. How could you?'

'I — I — ' she choked, incapable of going on.

'What on earth is the matter?'

She felt anger rise against him for his lack of understanding. Or possibly it was anger at her own inability to communicate. She turned on him, finding words at last. 'You — you idiot! I wanted to tell you something, but I can't! Oh, it's impossible!' She slapped his arm. 'Don't stare at me like that!'

'You're not makin' sense,' he protested. 'God, Cilla, if you've got somethin' to tell me, get on with it!'

'I — I can't!'

'Why? What in thunder is it?'

'Oh — it's — it's impossible! I thought I could, but you're in such an impatient mood . . . I can't! I can't!' And with that outburst, she fled. She ran back to the drapery store and darted inside. The door slammed shut, and Pete glared angrily at it. He wasn't entirely ignorant of a woman's moods, but this was the limit. What had the silly girl been trying to tell him? Probably it was some foolish thought, some idea she had. It was nice of her to believe that Harry hadn't committed murder, but her opinions would count for little.

He was tempted to walk into the store and try to mollify her, but a bone-weary feeling took possession of him. There was so much to do that he couldn't afford to waste his time on non essentials. He had to see his father and tell him the news. He had to get a lawyer, and that would probably entail a trip to Alpine. Sheriff Tom Sharkey had said a trial might be arranged within two days; if that was the case, time wasn't on his side.

Pete turned on his heel, still angry with the girl. He gathered up the leathers of the two TT mounts and walked them along to the livery stable close by. A fresh animal was a necessity, even for the short ride to the TT spread. He would hire one.

Some time elapsed before he came out of the stable with a fresh horse on which he had slipped a clean saddle-blanket and his own saddle. The word had gone around town that Harry Hadfield had been brought back by his brother. The news was passed around in stores, saloons, on the boardwalks, and even at the little mission church. There were many who thought this was justice. Some considered it strange for a man to bring back his own brother, and others said, 'There'll be a hangin'! Ain't been one in town for a hell of a long time . . . '

Pete was walking his fresh horse to the edge of town when he found himself passing Big Ben Link's black-smith's forge. The man was working at the anvil but he looked up as the shadow of the horse and rider fell across his threshold and he hailed Pete.

'Hey, young feller . . . is it true? You brought him back?'

'That's right.' Pete halted the animal.

Link walked over, hammer in hand, his black leather apron flapping against his big legs. 'You found him?'

'Yes, I found him,' Pete said curtly.

'Has he told you anything? I mean, did he kill that girl? Has he confessed?'

'He didn't kill her,' Pete gritted out. 'And I'm gonna prove it.'

Big Ben Link shook his head doubtfully. 'That's a touchin' show of faith in your own kin, but he was caught with that girl — and she was dead. Martha and Ted Smith caught him. How're you gonna deny their testimony? They've been tellin' folks all over town that Harry visited her in that room at night.'

'So did others visit Polly, it seems,' said Pete grimly.

The blacksmith nodded. 'To tell you the truth, Pete, I dunno about him killin' the girl like that . . . '

'Thanks, Ben.'

'I want to tell you somethin' else, too.

Did you know that your pa horse-whipped Wally Bliss in town the other day?'

'No. I ain't been told about that.'

'It's true. Whipped him but good! Seems there was a bit of an argument, Wally Bliss tried to cut your pa's buckboard harness . . . ' Link told Pete the rest of it, then he said, 'If I was you or your pa, I'd watch out for that nasty little runt. I hear he's been making the rounds of the saloons with Mick Laverty and they've been talkin' about how they aim to get even with your pa — and maybe you, too. Yeah, you're a Hadfield, boy.'

'I'm ridin' out to the TT right now.'

'Sure. Say, did Harry tell you who the galoot was who rode him away from that hangnoose party?'

'He didn't, Ben. But I aim to get at the truth pretty soon. This whole town is gonna learn that Harry did not kill that girl!'

He cantered out of the town and hit the east trail, his body hunched forward, reins held in gloved hands. He gave the fresh mount full rein, hearing the drumming hoofs as a sort of grim music. The animal was a dapple-grey, full of frisky energy and well-fed.

This time there was no attempt at murder as he passed the Comanche War Rocks. He saw only a distant rider picking his careful way down a shale-strewn slope. He cleared the last homestead where a woman in a fenced yard milked a cow and looked at him as he passed. Then he was on open range and headed for the TT spread.

He found his father and Sam Lacey near a well, testing the water. As Pete dismounted, Sam took the reins of the horse. Gilbert Hadfield sent a harsh, blank look at his son. 'Well?'

'He's in a cell,' Pete said.

Gilbert Hadfield heaved a sigh. 'I told you he'd be better off ridin' wild and free.'

'As a wanted man — wanted for murder?'

Sam Lacey said, 'I'll stable your

horse, Pete.' He led the animal away.

'Harry didn't kill that girl,' said Pete. He pulled off his gloves and beat dust from his vest and pants. 'We've got to start provin' he didn't do it.'

'Has he said he didn't kill her?' Gilbert Hadfield asked blandly.

'No. I still get a pack of nonsense from him. But I heard him talkin' in his sleep.'

The greying man rasped, 'Talkin' in his sleep? What did he say? Anyway, you can't place any reliance on that.'

'He was wounded. I had to shoot him to make him come back with me. The things he muttered in his sleep didn't make much sense — but I know he didn't kill that girl!'

'You shot him . . . ?' Lines deepened in the old man's face. 'How bad is he? Damn it, Pete, tell me everything!'

Pete Hadfield told his father about the ride to the tip of West Texas and of the encounter with the sheriff of Santa Arena, how the man had tried to hold him to ransom and how he had died.

'That was bad,' Pete added. 'I haven't told Tom Sharkey about it.'

'Then don't! Lawmen die by the dozen. It's a short life even for lucky ones. Anyhow, Santa Arena is a long way from here.'

'You don't put much value on human life, Pa!' Pete was surprised that he had made the outburst, but he went on, 'When that girl died, at first you figured it might be good for Harry if he came back and faced a trial — but then you decided he should ride wild and free. You don't seem concerned about the death of that girl. And you ain't rattled at all about the sheriff's death!'

'I saw good men die fast when I was young,' Gilbert Hadfield muttered. 'I quit worryin' over that sort of thing a long time ago. A dead galoot is just that — dead!'

'I hear you horse-whipped Wally Bliss,' Pete said.

'You heard right. Bliss is a damned low-down skunk.'

Pete turned. 'I figured you'd want to

hear everything, Pa. I'm gonna wash and change my clothes. I've been ridin', sleepin' and sweatin' in this rig. I'll be ridin' back to town tonight. I aim to talk to everybody. I want to know who rode Harry out that night of the lynch mob. Do you know he got back here and picked himself a TT mount?'

Gilbert Hadfield regarded his son with a scowl. 'Well, he knows his way around well enough.'

'Yeah. He also had money and one of our blankets. Plus a gun.'

'He should've made it to the border.' The scowl deepened. 'Are you gonna watch him swing?'

'Tomorrow I'll ride to Alpine and get defence counsel for Harry — after I've talked to every damn man in town about that masked rider who helped Harry.'

Pete walked determinedly away from his father. He bathed in a big trough in the bunkhouse, then he went to the ranchhouse and shaved. He got into clean black cord pants, a black cotton shirt and a brown deerskin vest, dumping his dirty clothes in the laundry basket. He even found an old but clean hat, a genuine J.B. stetson. He checked his gun, cleaned it quickly and slipped it back into his holster. Then he returned to the bunkhouse where he got the cook to rustle up some food. He was finishing the meal when he saw Sam Lacey enter the bunkhouse, his boots thumping dully on the bare boards. He said:

'Sam, do you remember tellin' me that Polly Bliss was real bad medicine?'

The ranch hand met his questioning eyes. 'Yeah, I guess I said that.'

'Did you ever meet her?'

Sam lowered his gaze. 'Yeah.'

'How did that come about?'

'I just talked to her. She was in the hardware store. She wasn't a saloon girl, you know.'

'No . . . folks wouldn't think she was so nice if she'd been a saloon girl,' Pete said sharply. 'Was that the only time you met her, Sam?'

'Nope — I saw her once again.' The other man jerked. 'Hey, what are you tryin' to say?'

'I'm just asking about that girl. I'm goin' into town tonight and I'm gonna ask a thousand questions and I might even get one or two good answers. When did you see Polly Bliss again?'

'You can go to hell, Pete Hadfield,' said Sam Lacey hotly. 'If you think I'd fool with her, you're plumb wrong.'

'Just tell me about the second time, Sam . . . '

The other man turned his back.

'You never had much to do with women, Sam,' said Pete grimly. 'Or maybe you like to let people think you're that way. Did you know that girl? Come clean, Sam.'

Sam Lacey faced Pete again, his eyes blazing. 'Boss's son or not, you don't talk to me like that!'

'Sam, I've got to know all about that girl!'

'Then know this!' Sam Lacey's fist rammed out as he lost himself to anger.

The blow hit Pete Hadfield on the chin. Pete staggered back, caught his balance, and came at Sam, fists raised.

Then Pete halted and slowly lowered his fists. He licked at his dry lips and found words. 'Sorry . . . I'm just as ornery as a loco steer about this affair . . . '

Sam Lacey stared into Pete's eyes for some moments and then he turned on his heel and left the bunkhouse. Pete Hadfield sighed, bunched his fists and stood statue-still for some seconds, wondering if he would succeed in helping Harry. All his actions so far seemed only to stir up trouble. He had insulted Sam Lacey more or less deliberately, trying to penetrate the man's mind. Somehow he felt that Sam nursed secret thoughts about the dead girl. It was just a feeling he had, nebulous and uncertain. But maybe it wasn't even important, this scrap, this ounce of knowledge that Sam carried in his mind.

Pete walked slowly from the bunk-house debating whether he should ride back to town immediately. He would get the dapple-grey and arm himself with a rifle.

He was pretty sure he wouldn't need his bedroll or water canteen for this night's activities. He would ride fast, and by hell, he'd stir up something in town! Somewhere, surely, was some man who knew the identity of the rider who had plucked Harry from the buckboard under the hanging tree. Harry knew, but how could he be made to talk? Maybe he would when the trial started, but maybe it would be too late. One thing was certain: if Harry hadn't killed Polly Bliss, then some low skunk in Perkinsville was the guilty man. His mind made up on a course of action, Pete Hadfield swung towards the stables. He was walking past the cottonwoods when he heard the sound of a horse and the squeak of buggy springs. Looking around, he saw a moving shape on the track that wound down to the TT gates. A buggy driven by a girl! Momentarily later he saw that it was Cilla Gregg.

He waited until the rig rolled into the ranchyard and the horse came to a halt, snorting and tossing its head. 'What brings you here, Cilla?'

'Aren't you glad to see me?'

'Why, sure,' he said hastily. 'I'm sorry I was so rude to you back in town.' He helped her down. One thing Pete did know about girls was that you had to be mighty polite and courteous with them, even to the extent of handing out extravagant flattery. He tried it. 'You — you look great, Cilla.'

'And you're a great deal more presentable than you looked two hours ago.'

He smiled faintly. 'What brings you out here, Cilla? Do you have something on your mind?'

'I have.' She touched his arm. 'Oh, Pete, I just had to have a talk with you. I know you'll never believe this, but it's true. Oh, I'll have to start at the beginning. Dear Pete, I don't want to hurt you — but I know who killed Polly Bliss!'

'You? How can you know anything about a girl like that?'

'I'm friendly with Curly. Do you know him? The Indian boy. He's a deaf mute, poor boy. Well, he knows who killed Polly Bliss. He saw it happen and it frightened him terribly. He's at the sheriff's office right now. I want you to come into town, Pete, and — '

At that moment two rifles cracked from a rocky defile and the bullets spat into the ground close to Pete and the girl. He grabbed her arm and raced her back to the ranch house. As they ran, the rifles cracked again and the slugs whined through the air over their heads.

10

Death Cancels Everything

Inside the ranch house, with the door rammed shut behind them, Pete whipped to a window and carefully looked out. There was no movement on the broken, rocky ground to the left of the trail into the TT ranch yard. But men were there, hidden. He figured he'd heard two rifles in action. If they had intended to kill him or Cilla, their aim hadn't been too good.

As he stared out, his father entered the living room, his big strides taking him to the window beside his son. 'What in tarnation is goin' on? Who's out there?'

'Some jaspers who don't like us, Pa!' Pete moved away, taking care not to show himself at the window. Rifles were stored in an old mahogany case near the fireplace. They were oiled and clean and ready to take shells. Pete got out two guns and handed one to his father just as Sam Lacey burst into the room.

'Who the hell's doin' all that shootin'?' He sucked in his breath when he saw the girl. 'Sorry, Miss Gregg.'

She smiled faintly. She had come out to the ranch to tell Pete everything she had discovered just as she had already told the sheriff. She knew it would be difficult to find the right words, just as it had proved to be almost impossible to get Sheriff Tom Sharkey to believe her tale. In fact, the sheriff had been more than just obstinate, refusing to accept the difficult task of communicating with Curly, the Kiowa boy. She had left Curly with the sheriff after Curly had made scores of strange symbols and drawings in the office, compelling the sheriff to cudgel his brains. Now, staring in fear, her eyes large in her chalk-white face, she knew she couldn't talk unless she was alone with Pete. She couldn't say the terrible things she had to say — not with his father and Sam Lacey in the room.

'There are three of us,' said Sam Lacey. 'We'll get them bushwhackers! A pity the hands are out by the waterholes and mendin' fences. Only the cook is here, but I ain't askin' him to tote a gun.'

'Pin them down with rifle-fire,' said Pete. 'I'll go out the back way and circle those rocks. Maybe I can get 'em from the other side.'

'Know who's behind them guns?' said Gilbert Hadfield grimly.

'I've got a pretty good idea,' said Pete. 'I've been told that Wally Bliss and Mick Laverty have got it in for us Hadfields.'

'That runty little drifter!'

'Could be him,' Pete said. 'And Laverty hates us. I bested him in a fight and Harry took Polly Bliss from him, or so Laverty believes. As for Wally Bliss, he's sure Harry killed his sister.'

'That damned girl! I'm sick and tired of hearin' her name!' Gilbert Hadfield thundered. 'Will you just shut up about her, Pete? I don't want any more talk like that in this house!'

'All this trouble is over that girl,' said Sam Lacey slowly.

Gilbert Hadfield jerked around to him. 'Didn't you hear? I'm damned sick of hearin' that girl's name!'

'Your son is in a cell because of that girl,' Sam said. 'He should be ridin' wide and free, by heaven!'

The big man turned again, this time to face Pete. 'You had to poke into it! Harry's the kind to go wild in any case! But you didn't understand that. Why didn't you stay out of it, Pete?'

'I'll clear him, Pa. Just you see — his name will be cleared!'

A hard, harsh mask settled down on Gilbert Hadfield's face as he gripped his rifle. Cilla stared at him in fascination. Sam Lacey wore a bland expression but his hands were knotted into fists.

'I'm goin' out there!' Gilbert Hadfield shouted suddenly. 'By thunder, I'll teach that Bliss runt to come gunnin' around here! This is my range and I run it!'

'I'll go, Pa.' Pete moved to the door. 'I'll flush 'em out.'

'You can damned well stay right here!' roared the older man, his face suffused with rage. 'I'll kill them like I'd destroy varmints! I don't need you, Pete! I can handle this just like I can handle anything else! You should've realized that!'

'I don't know what you're gettin' at, Pa!'

'I'm tellin' you that you shouldn't have stuck your nose into all this. Harry's in that jail because you put him there — your own brother! You had to go out and hunt him down! I told you to let him take his chance. He'd have been fine — free — ridin' where he wants, but you had to horn in!'

'It was you who told me to bring him in.'

'That was before I had time to think about it. When he got away from that

184

lynch mob, that was the time to let him go. Hell, the country is full of wanted jaspers hitting the trails.'

'As wanted men — outlaws — usin' their guns against decent people,' Pete said. 'I agree it's only natural to run for survival — but not when a man is innocent!'

At that moment rifles cracked and glass splintered in the ranch house living room. Raging, raucous shouts were heard, slurred into almost meaningless cries by anger and whisky. Sam Lacey and Gilbert Hadfield moved to the broken window, gripping their rifles and sliding shells into the magazines. Pete took Cilla's arm and led her to the far side of the room. With a heave he upended a heavy old mahogany table and told her to stay behind it.

'You'll be all right there, Cilla. I'll make those hellions pay for this. Just stay put, honey.'

'Oh, Pete, I wanted to tell you about Harry! About the scene Curly witnessed! He saw — '

'Later, Cilla . . . let's deal with those two fools out there first. I bet they've been drinkin'!'

With this comment he slipped away from the girl. He took one glance at Sam Lacey and his father beside the window and then he darted to the rear of the ranch house. As he moved, he heard their guns boom.

He went around the house, paused and then ran for the shelter of the cottonwoods, cradling his rifle. He hit the shelter of the first tree bole as a bullet whined through the air a few feet wide of him. He smiled thinly, remembering Mick Laverty's poor marksmanship.

Then he heard wild threats from the two men and knew they were filled with more than just hate. They had been at the cheap booze sold in Sal's Place, a fiery, cut-price rotgut made in a local still.

'We aim to get you, Hadfield! Your rotten brother will hang and we'll get you!' It was Mick Laverty's voice. He and the other gunhand were behind cover in the rough ground just off the approach trail to the TT gates.

'You're a fool, Laverty!' Pete shouted back. 'Hightail it for town, you loco bum! If you make another crazy play with those guns, you'll likely stop lead. There are three of us here!'

'You don't scare me none!' Laverty answered. 'I hate you and your brother. He'll hang and you'll die. You bested me in a fight and made me look like a fool!'

'You were lucky at the Comanche War Rocks!' Pete shouted. 'Don't chance it again! Get goin'! I'm warnin' you!'

Another voice screamed through the air. 'We're gonna kill you and then we'll burn that fancy house right down to the ground! I'll watch that damned father of yours sizzle. No man whips me!' It was Wally Bliss.

'I'll give you one more chance,' Pete shouted. 'Get goin'. Get on your horses, ride, and cool off!'

His answer was a barrage of shots that spattered the earth around the cottonwood bole. At the same time shots blasted from the ranch house window, but there were no cries of pain to indicate that a bullet had found a target. Assuming that the two men in the rocky draw were reloading their weapons, Pete snapped off two shots, just to let them know he was still around more than anything else because he couldn't see any movement. He knew he would have to circle them to get them in sight. And now was the time to do it — if they were reloading.

He sprinted, head down, behind the bunkhouse building, then to the pole corral, diving to earth behind the skimpy cover of a main post. The guns in the house were firing.

Evidently Sam Lacey and his father were watching his progress. And maybe Mick Laverty and Wally Bliss were trying to get him in their sights. There wasn't much to worry about with Laverty, but Wally Bliss could be a good shot with a rifle for all Pete knew.

They were two drunken fools, but they were dangerous. Any fool with a gun was dangerous.

He thought fleetingly about Cilla. She had something to tell him about Harry — something about an Indian boy and a scene he'd witnessed. It would have to wait, but maybe she had some scrap of information that could help Harry. It must be important because she had gone to the sheriff . . .

Shots rang out and he had to concentrate his thoughts in another direction. His shelter was scanty. They might get a bead on him.

He figured he'd go behind them, line his rifle on them and demand that they drop their guns. He'd give them one chance. If they didn't take it . . .

He ran again and reached a shallow gully just high enough to cover him as he moved forward at a crouch. The gully brought him right behind the two men in the rocks. They heard his onward rush and pumped bullets wildly, but he kept his head down. He had, he knew, lost the chance to get the drop on them. He could leap up and fire, but it was two to one.

He hugged the ground just below the rim of the shallow gully. He knew the other two men were facing him now instead of the ranch house, keeping to their cover.

The setup was a bit tricky and one false move might be fatal. But sooner or later someone would have to make a play.

The move came from the ranch house, a reckless act on Gilbert Hadfield's part. He came running across the yard, his gun blazing at the yellow rocks. Behind him Sam Lacey stood at the ranch house door, his face a set mask, his rifle ready.

As Gilbert Hadfield ran forward he shouted, 'You dirty scum! You dare to come here shootin' my place up! By God, I'll teach you that a Hadfield is worth ten of you!'

At that moment Wally Bliss stood up

and levelled his gun. It wasn't an easy shot but his target was a big man.

Two slugs fired in rapid succession took the big rancher in the chest. He crumpled as if the bone in his legs had turned to jelly. He fell face forward, then raised himself with his arms. His gun had been thrown to one side. He tried to claw himself along the ground. Pete stared in momentary disbelief, then turned and fired at Wally Bliss.

The small man was thrown back by the impact of the bullet. At that, Mick Laverty crawled out of the hole in which he had been hiding, his face ashen under the dirt, his hands high in the air.

Pete ran to his father, threw his gun to the side and raised the big rancher from the ground. Two red holes stained Gilbert Hadfield's shirt. Blood pumped out at a terrible rate and spilled over Pete's hands. Sam Lacey came running, his gun at the ready, held hip-high.

'Listen, Pete, and listen good . . . ' Gilbert Hadfield's eyes were over-bright and his face was contorted with agony. 'Harry didn't kill the girl,' Hadfield said. 'I'm tellin' you now because I . . . I'm gonna die. Should have told you . . . truth . . . long ago . . . figured Harry was hell-bent in any case! Listen, son . . . ain't much time . . . '

He coughed, then licked his lips with a tongue that was flecked with bloodied froth. 'I killed that girl . . . Harry knew it . . . figured to take . . . blame . . . young fool . . . '

'You? No, Pa! That — that's impossible!'

'You're too decent, son, to really understand . . . I visited Polly Bliss . . . don't — don't turn from me . . . not now . . . she taunted me . . . called me an old man . . . I — I — was just lonely, Pete . . . lonely . . . I — I strangled her . . . lost my head . . . blacked out . . . '

'But, Harry — '

'Yeah . . . he got there right after I left her. He . . . he . . . passed me in that dark alley . . . I saw him look . . . I hurried away . . . Harry guessed the rest. People never knew I'd been to that room . . . God — I only went there twice . . . '

'You knew he was innocent? You wanted him to take the blame?'

'He — he talked to me . . . that night . . . rode out . . . I thought to get him back and I'd confess . . . but then I figured he was wild. It was me who rode him away from . . . lynch mob . . . gave him . . . horse . . . money . . . gun . . . '

Pete held the big man, rocking him as if he were a child. 'Pa — it doesn't matter. Do you understand? It don't matter . . . ' Pete looked up, into Sam Lacey's lined face.

'I guessed,' said Sam quietly. 'I knew he'd been with the girl. One night in town I saw his horse hitched near that alley. Thought no more about it until the night I came quietly into the ranch house and heard him muttering in some sort of agony . . . remorse, I guess. I just heard him mention her name. It was the night she got killed.'

They tried to lift Gilbert Hadfield

but a cry came from his throat and they lowered him back. Then he was dead. Pete Hadfield put bloody hands to his face and felt ill. Sam Lacey breathed hard and looked down at the silent Mick Laverty, his mouth twisting.

Later they carried the dead rancher back to the house and placed him on a bed. Cilla swayed with shock.

'Oh, Pete, how can I tell you?'

'I know what that Indian boy saw,' Pete said quietly. 'Pa confessed — and God rest his soul.'

Cilla told him how Curly had climbed the outside staircase to the window of the girl's room, fascinated in an adolescent way by the strange activities in the room. He had seen the girl strangled. Then he saw Gilbert Hadfield leaving and Harry Hadfield arriving.

Pete had to console her when she broke down. She was still in his arms when Tom Sharkey came riding in with a newly sworn deputy, to tell Pete that the Indian boy's account would be checked by an expert with deaf and dumb children. He heard the story of Gilbert Hadfield's dying confession with a stern face.

'Ain't for me to judge,' he said gently, 'but your pa is dead now and let's leave it at that. There'll be a hearin', of course, but I reckon Harry's in the clear.'

The next day, Pete told the sheriff about Chet Lancer. A week later, Tom Sharkey called Pete to his office and said, 'Santa Arena never had a sheriff. That galoot was an outlaw. Seems he had a yen to wear a badge. He just bullied the folks in that town into lettin' him be sheriff. Imagine that! He even had a price on his head!'

A month later Pete and Cilla were making plans for their wedding. Harry would be the best man.

'Funny,' remarked Pete, 'but he's not so wild now.'

'Well,' said Cilla happily, 'he can unbend a little at our wedding.'

We do hope that you have enjoyed reading this large print book.

Did you know that all of our titles are available for purchase?

We publish a wide range of high quality large print books including:
**Romances, Mysteries, Classics
General Fiction
Non Fiction and Westerns**

Special interest titles available in large print are:
**The Little Oxford Dictionary
Music Book, Song Book
Hymn Book, Service Book**

Also available from us courtesy of Oxford University Press:
**Young Readers' Dictionary
(large print edition)
Young Readers' Thesaurus
(large print edition)**

For further information or a free brochure, please contact us at:
**Ulverscroft Large Print Books Ltd.,
The Green, Bradgate Road, Anstey,
Leicester, LE7 7FU, England.
Tel:** (00 44) **0116 236 4325**
Fax: (00 44) **0116 234 0205**

Other titles in the
Linford Western Library:

SMOKING STAR

B. J. Holmes

In the one-horse town of Medicine Bluff two men were dead. Sheriff Jack Starr didn't need the badge on his chest to spur him into tracking the killer. He had his own reason for seeking justice, a reason no-one knew. It drove him to take a journey into the past where he was to discover something else that was to add even greater urgency to the situation — to stop Montana's rivers running red with blood.

THE WIND WAGON

Troy Howard

Sheriff Al Corning was as tough as they came and with his four seasoned deputies he kept the peace in Laramie — at least until the squatters came. To fend off starvation, the settlers took some cattle off the cowmen, including Jonas Lefler. A hard, unforgiving man, Lefler retaliated with lynchings. Things got worse when one of the squatters revealed he was a former Texas lawman — and no mean shooter. Could Sheriff Corning prevent further bloodshed?

CABEL

Paul K. McAfee

Josh Cabel returned home from the Civil War to find his family all murdered by rioting members of Quantrill's band. The hunt for the killers led Josh to Colorado City where, after months of searching, he finally settled down to work on a ranch nearby. He saved the life of an Indian, who led him to a cache of weapons waiting for Sitting Bull's attack on the Whites. His involvement threw Cabel into grave danger. When the final confrontation came, who had the fastest — and deadlier — draw?

RIVERBOAT

Alan C. Porter

When Rufus Blake died he was found to be carrying a gold bar from a Confederate gold shipment that had disappeared twenty years before. This inspires Wes Hardiman and Ben Travis to swap horse and trail for a riverboat, the *River Queen*, on the Mississippi, in an effort to find the missing gold. Cord Duval is set on destroying the *River Queen* and he has the power and the gunmen to do it. Guns blaze as Hardiman and Travis attempt to unravel the mystery and stay alive.

McKINNEY'S LAW

Mike Stotter

McKinney didn't count on coming across a dead body in the middle of Texas. He was about to become involved in an ever-deepening mystery. The renegade Comanche warrior, Black Eagle, was on the loose, creating havoc; he didn't appear in McKinney's plans at all, not until the Comanche forced himself into his life. The US Army gave McKinney some relief to his problems, but it also added to them, and with two old friends McKinney set about bringing justice through his own law.

BLACK RIVER

Adam Wright

John Dyer has come to the insignificant little town of Black River to destroy the last living reminder of his dark past. He has come to kill. Jack Hart is determined to stop him. Only he knows the terrible truth that has driven Dyer here, and he knows that only he can beat Dyer in a gunfight. Ex-lawman Brad Harris is after Dyer too — to avenge his family. The stage is set for madness, death and vengeance.